Saving HER

SHE CRIES TO BREAK FREE

SOFIIA DAVIID

To every victim of abuse

Saving

HER

SHE CRIES TO BREAK FREE

The world breaks everyone, and afterward, many are strong at the broken places.

-Ernest Hemingway

Lagos

Prologue

I didn't like him, the way he looked at me and the way he treated mum, he always made me uncomfortable. I told my mum how I felt, but all she did was flag me down and tell me to shut up because I was too young to know anything. They were getting married today and for the life of me, I couldn't understand why I had a terrible feeling about it. It felt wrong.

I preferred her other boyfriend, uncle Jaxon. He was sweeter and more interesting. He always took me out, bought me ice cream, and played games with me. I loved and missed the way he used to comb my hair and braid it whenever mum wasn't around. Whenever I was running late and couldn't meet up with the bus, he would take me to school. He lived with us for a while, but then suddenly he disappeared. He stopped coming over and he stopped calling.

When I asked mum where he was, all she said was, 'he's away.' I waited for him to come back and take me out to the places he promised we would go to but hadn't. A day turned to a week, a month, then a year, and I knew he was never coming back.

One day when I missed him, I waited till my mother was asleep before I took her phone to call him. I couldn't identify what she saved his number with, so I dialed it offhand. I still remembered when he made me memorize his number for cases of emergencies, and at that moment I was happy that I knew it.

He picked the call on the second ring and his voice was groggy but I could still detect the confusion in it.

"Dianne?" His voice was just as I had remembered, deep and there was something about it that made me at peace.

"Uncle Jaxon, it's Funke," I whispered so mum wouldn't hear me. She was sleeping in the living room while I was upstairs in my room.

"Funke? Is everything okay? Where's your mum?" His voice was sharper and more awake now.

"She's fine. Are you fine? I miss you. I've been waiting for you since and you still haven't come." My eyes stung as tears welled up.

He sighed heavily. "I'm fine Funke, I just have to be away for now." His voice was a mix of relief and sadness. I couldn't pin it. "How have you been? I miss you too."

"Ever since you left, things have been different. Mum hardly has time for me anymore and there's no one to play with but Ayanda." I let the tears fall as I spoke. "And she's boring," I added.

He chuckled. "You know what? I will come over soon."

"Really?" My spirits lifted with hope and I sniffled. "You're coming?"

"Yes, I'm coming Funke. We'll going to go out together, I'll buy you ice cream and we'll watch your favorite movies," I could imagine the huge smile on his face now and that gave me a reason to smile.

"And you'll braid my hair?" I added.

"And I'll braid your hair," he chuckled. "So tell me, how is school? How many new friends have you made?"

And I told him everything. My new friends, both girls, boys, and the ones I didn't like. We talked till my mother knocked on the door of my room and asked for her phone. Before he ended the call, he once again promised to see me soon. I deleted the call log because I didn't want mum to see it and have a reason to be mad at me.

Exactly two months after that, mum came home with a man I had never seen in my life. She told me she was going to get married to him and he was going to be my father.

From the moment I set my eyes on him, I knew he was of no good. *"His name is Seyi, and he works with Shell"* mum had told me. That still didn't make me like him. From day one, every cell in my body hated him.

Two months after she introduced me to Seyi, we were both wearing white dresses, and her make-up was nicely done. She looked really beautiful as she stared at herself in the mirror. She smiled down at me, took my hand in hers, and turned to face me.

SAVING HER

"You'll always be my baby and no one is going to change that fact, not even Seyi." Her smile widened. "I love you," she pulled me into a hug.

"I love you too," I accepted her embrace wholeheartedly.

Few minutes after, she was walking down the aisle with me in front of her, and uncle Dayo, her younger brother by her side with her clutching his arm. That was the first time I was seeing him and the rest of mum's family. I heard about them once in a blue moon, but this was the first time I was meeting them. None of them bothered to talk to me and I didn't bother to either.

I watched mum and Seyi as they exchanged vows and the moment mum had said *I do,* my world came crashing down. At the reception, I watched everyone having fun, all but me. Sitting down for so long made my butt hurt, so I begged mum's chief bridesmaid to help me unlock my mother's car and wind down all the glasses. I could do it by myself, but no one would let me. The only reason she allowed me to go to the car was that her boyfriend had his car parked right beside mum's and he was in the car so I wasn't technically on my own.

13

After five minutes in the car with my eyes closed, I opened them again, and I had to rub them to be sure I was seeing correctly. Uncle Jaxon was walking towards the car, and without thinking, I jumped down from the car and ran to him. I threw myself on him and he caught me with ease, a hearty laugh escaping his lips.

"You came!" I screamed, not caring that people were around us.

"I told you I will." He didn't let go of me and I didn't either.

I missed him so much and at that moment I didn't care that my mother had just gotten married to a man I didn't like. All that mattered was that Uncle Jaxon was there, and that was enough for me.

Moments after, he dropped me to the ground and I still couldn't stop smiling. "What took you so long?"

"Work, I've been busy." I noted what he was wearing. A nice suit, or maybe it was a tuxedo that made him more attractive.

Mum, what went wrong?

"I'm just so happy you're here." I hugged him again, this time with my feet planted firmly on the ground.

"Come on, I brought something for you." He took mum's car keys from the chief bridesmaid who knew him, wounded up the glasses in the car and locked the doors before dragging me with him to his car. He told me to sit in the passenger's seat of his fully tinted Range Rover, turned on the car and the air conditioning before he got down to get something out of the trunk of the car. When he got back into the car, he gave me a gift bag. I was about to open it, but he stopped me. "No, when you get home."

I smiled, "okay."

We both sat in the car, the engine running, as we talked. I once again told him everything. He found a few things I said funny, successfully mocking me and advising me when he had to. As we spoke in the car, I couldn't help but imagine him as my father and not Seyi. My life would have made more sense if he were my mother's husband. I wouldn't mind calling him 'dad' even though I knew he was not my biological father.

Speaking of biological fathers, I was oblivious to who or where mine was, but I was cool with it because my life was good enough without him. Though I wished he was there but that was that. With Uncle Jaxon, he made me want to have someone to call 'dad.'

A loud knocking on the driver's window startled me, and I screamed in shock. Uncle Jaxon was just as shocked as I was because his hand was over his chest as he looked outside the window at my fuming mother.

He got down from the car and I followed suit.

"What the fuck are you doing here? No, what the hell are you doing? With my daughter?" Mum's eyes flickered to mine, and she marched to the side of the car I was at and held me by my wrist, pulling me away from Uncle Jaxon and the car.

He ran his hand through his dreadlocks and sighed. "You know I won't do shit like that Dianne." He took a few steps toward us and I expected mum to withdraw but she didn't. "Look, we were just talking alright?" He looked at me as if waiting for me to say something in his defense.

"Yes mum, we were just talking," I said and looked at her.

She wanted to speak again, but she held her tongue and sighed before letting go of my wrist. "I trust you, Jaxon," she said to him, and he nodded.

16

SAVING HER

We both watched mum walk into the reception hall and only until she was out of sight did I look back at Uncle Jaxon.

"Want to get ice cream?" His face changed to the way it was before mum had come over.

"Yes," and like that, I forgot about mum and Uncle Jaxon's banter mere seconds ago.

Lagos

Chapter One

This was it, the moment I had been waiting for most of my life. I was tired of being abused and used like I didn't matter to anyone, so this was where I was drawing the line.

My stepfather had abused me from day one. He had raped me, beaten me up, and forced me to sleep on the cold floor with no form of protection from the cold. I had gotten pregnant, and he had pushed me to go for an abortion, not once, not twice. To worsen it, my mother, the person who was supposed to be my confidant, my number one person didn't know about all this, or rather she ignored the topic, always changing it as fast as she could whenever I brought it up. She believed I hated him. Well, she was right. I hated him.

SAVING HER

Because of her abnormal work schedule, she was never in town, always on one business trip or the other, leaving me in the hands of my stepfather for him to use me as he pleased.

My stepfather was smart enough to not get caught: Two weeks before my mother would come home, he wouldn't beat me or physically hurt me, always taking that time to rape and verbally abuse me. If there were scars on my body, I had to come up with stupid excuses to explain their existence if my mother noticed them there.

It all started when I was twelve and that was when puberty hit me hard. My period started for the first time when I was in school and since my mother was non-existent, my teacher filled that role for me. New to the whole thing, it was like I was growing all over again. I looked bigger in obvious places and with the monthly visitor came pimples and mood swings.

I think it was the fact that I was still *fresh and ripe,* as they called it, that heightened his senses. He used to physically and emotionally abuse me before, but that was the beginning of the sexual abuse. It started with him coming into my room when he knew I was getting dressed and since I'd be half-naked or even naked at that point, he'd tell me to stand still. He would walk around me like an eagle, sampling its prey before attacking.

The first time this happened, he didn't say or do anything before he left the room. I cried so much that night, but what could I have done? The second time, I attempted to lock my door, and I thought I was safe, but boy was I wrong. The moment I stepped out of the bathroom, he knocked the door down and, like a deer caught in head's light; I stood there, frozen. This time around, he tried to touch me, but I pushed his hand away. He left my room laughing.

He refused to fix my door back and to worsen it; he took away the broken door to God knows where. I tried changing rooms, but he locked all the rooms in the house and hid the keys, leaving me in a room that lacked privacy. I thought hard and came up with an idea: I took my old blanket, put together some ropes and sticks, and hung the blanket around the door frame like a curtain. When he came back from work and saw my little work, he tore the blanket to shreds, took it outside, and set it ablaze. I watched in horror as it turned to ashes.

SAVING HER

I couldn't help the tears that ran down my face and the sobs that broke through me. He stood outside till everything about the blanket was gone and the fire was out. From my window, I watched him disappear from the compound and reappear at my doorway. The sight of him startled me and I jumped up in fear. He slowly walked toward me and laughed. I begged him not to do whatever it was, but it was like he was being controlled. Before I could comprehend what was going on, he pounced on me like a lion attacking its prey.

I trashed, pushed, bit, and screamed, but he was persistent in having his way with me. Everywhere he touched me felt like my skin was on fire, I felt like cutting my skin from my body. He ripped my clothes; I had never felt that helpless in my life. When he was done with what he wanted to do, he beat me up and left me bloodied on the floor. I cried my eyes out that night, not because he had his way with me, but because I knew that wasn't the end. It was bound to happen again, and I didn't know how long, but I was positive for the next three months until my mother came back from her trip. I hadn't lost my virginity that day and I already felt that was the worst. If that was how being touched without my consent felt, then how would it be if he had gotten the last bit of my innocence?

After that day, it got worse. I gave up protesting and screaming because I knew nothing was going to happen. He sometimes insisted that I walked around the house in my birthday suit just for his entertainment. My life no longer felt like mine.

For those three months before my mother got back from her trip, he didn't rip me off of my last bit of innocence, but the beatings were horrible.

When my mother got back, he acted like nothing had happened. He threatened that if I told my mother; he was going to kill us both so I kept my mouth shut. My wounds had healed before her return, leaving faint scars in their place, which she failed to notice. I prayed that would be the end, but I was wrong. It had only just begun.

Before I jumped out the window, I took a last look at my room and put my bag pack over my shoulders. For a while now, I had been secretly practicing my escape from this house.

I landed noiselessly on the interlocking of the compound and did a quick scan of the area to be sure the coast was clear before making a run for it. I had pushed aside the electrical wires hung on the fence to make my escape easier.

Where I was running off to, I didn't know, but my determination to leave the house for good was at its peak. I had endured enough. With one jump I was hanging on the fence and I balanced my weight to get a good grip on the fence. I already had one leg over when suddenly my environment became brighter.

Shit, I have to leave now.

As I was swinging my second leg over, the sound of a gunshot had me bending forward and almost losing my balance. I gripped the fence hard to keep steady. My stepfather's maniacal laugh had me turning to him. His Glock-19 pistol was in his hand, smoke escaping the muzzle with a wicked smile on his face. Like in the movies I had watched, he blew air on the muzzle and I watched as the smoke floated in the air's direction from his mouth.

"I don't think I need to tell you what is going to happen if you don't get down from there."

I shivered as his words shook my entire being. He was going to shoot me and I could die from it. I sat on the fence, weighing my options and thinking of the best way to get out of this. His eyes remained on me, carefully waiting for my next move. I knew there was no escaping at that point.

I reluctantly pulled my other leg back to the other side of the fence and jumped down. Slowly walking toward the house, I knew what was going to happen next and for the first time in years; I wasn't ready for it.

Chicago

Chapter Two

I feel something tickle my face and I reach out to touch it. My tears are spilling over and my hands are shaking as I hold them in front of me. No matter how much I wish for it to stop, it doesn't and it most likely never will. I squeeze my palms together, trying to stop the shaking, but it only gets worse. My breath hitches in my throat and I clutch my neck. With every passing second, it is getting harder to breathe. They call it a panic attack and they say that I will get better, but a part of me never believes them. I am damaged, damaged beyond repair.

The door to the room I am in opens and someone walks in. I don't look up, but when his cologne hits my nose, I instantly know who it is, and he confirms it by calling my name. His voice is barely audible, but I hear him. I slowly lift my head to look at him and his brown eyes are the first things I see. They are like two drops of black coffee in a sea of milk, so mesmerizing.

His lips are moving, but I don't hear him or anything else but the deafening silence. His eyes scan my face with fear on his and he pries my hand from my neck and holds them in between his larger ones. He has bags under his eyes, his milk skin unable to hide the fact that he hasn't been sleeping properly, which makes me worry about him and intensifies my guilt. His lack of sleep is because of me. My PTSD (Post Traumatic Stress Disorder) has everyone on the edge, myself included. I do not know how I am going to cope for the next years of my life.

"Funke." He calls and this time around, I can hear him.

I blink once, then again, "Adrian," my voice is barely a whisper.

He pulls me to his chest and wraps his arms around my now slimmer figure. I'm naturally not like this, but in the past month of not eating, I have lost a few pounds. Everyone is worried, worried that I will develop once again another sickness: Ulcer. I worry about myself too.

My shaking finally stops and my head is resting safely on Adrian's chest, the rapid movement of his chest slowing down and comforting me in some manner. I don't know how long we are on the wooded floor but by the time I look up again, the sky which I last saw as a dull blue is now completely dark, the stars and the moon taking their place in the sky like chandeliers.

"Funke," Adrian says softly, placing his finger under my chin and pulling my face to look at his. "Are you okay?'

I nod and let out a breath.

He sighs, "I was so scared Funke, please stop scaring me. I know you can't help it, but please try."

He sighs in frustration when I pull away from him and stand up from the floor. I am doing everything they are asking me to do: going to the therapist, taking my medications, having interactions with people that aren't Adrian, his mother, or my mother, and forcing food into my stomach and not having to throw it out minutes after. I am doing more than I ever imagined, so why should they ask me to do something I have no control over?

I don't reply but simply walk to the door, ready to get out of this place. I need air. Adrian's form suddenly appears in front of me just when I reach for the doorknob.

"Look Funke, I'm sorry I didn't mean it like that," he apologizes, his eyes pleading with me.

"I know, just... excuse me," I tear my gaze away from his handsome face, not wanting to forget what is at hand.

He obeys, and the white door is once again in my line of sight. I turn the knob of the door, and a second after, my feet are moving across the wooden floor of the small house we are living in. This isn't Nigeria anymore, this is Chicago. When we moved from Nigeria a little over a month ago–after they sentenced my stepfather to jail–the plan was to have a yearlong vacation with which I could learn to live with PTSD and interact with people that aren't my family or Adrian. I knew it would not be possible, but I agreed because I needed to get away from my horrid past, and everything that had to do with it which meant leaving Nigeria and everything I once held dearly behind. It was a change, and change is something I'm slowly getting accustomed to.

SAVING HER

When we newly arrived in Chicago, we got a house close to the beach and the plan was to stay there for a month before moving to this house. They wanted me to have a little fun, experience the Chicago sun on my melanin skin, wear a bikini and dive into the ocean, and simply play my sorrows away, but I wasn't having it. After three weeks of trying, they gave up and agreed it was time to move. My mother pulled a few strings and got me and Adrian a job in a small store. We work Mondays to Fridays, from eight in the morning to one in the afternoon. It is a cool job and I enjoy working at the store. It has become my favorite thing to do in one week.

The slight breeze hits my face as I step out of the house and close the door behind me. My legs feel exposed at the moment because I'm not used to wearing shorts since our weather in Nigeria doesn't always support it, plus our morals, which have a slight mix of religion, but Chicago is different. I almost feel like a different person here.

It is a Saturday evening so I have no work and duties to attend to at the moment. I enjoy taking walks around the neighborhood, especially when it gets too hard to breathe inside the house. A few people already know me for my short walks around, from the house to the park and back. The park isn't too far away, so I'm not exactly stressing myself.

The evening breeze is cooler than the previous days as expected because summer is slowly ending and a part of me gets sad at the thought of it. My fun has just begun, but my flashbacks and panic attacks are getting worse. I have a frown on my face because of the thought of it. The flashbacks are horrible and I feel like a part of my soul gets chipped away with every resurface of a memory. The doctors say it is going to be a regular thing, but I can overcome it. I hope their words are true.

"Funke!" I turn around to find Adria jogging towards me, his hair a slight mess from tugging at it so much. He belongs here because his skin color is the same as the majority over here and I am a different person; my melanin skin makes the difference. This only applies to right now because the moment we step on Nigerian soil, the roles change.

Adrian is my best friend and I'm ever grateful for that. He's my savior and if not for him, I would have ended my life a long time ago.

SAVING HER

"Hey, can I walk with you?" He asks as he comes to a halt beside me.

"Sure," I nod and continue my walk with him now beside me.

This is familiar ground and a small smile stretches on my lips for the first time in a while now.

Lagos

Chapter Three

"I'm surprised to see you here," Adrian sarcastically said as he settled himself on his seat beside me. School had started an hour ago, and he had just arrived, but I didn't have the strength to question him.

Yesterday I told him I would run away and he shouldn't expect me in school the next day. He didn't believe that I could go through with it. I slightly turned my head to look at him, and he flinched, shocked to see my face like that.

"What the fuck happened to you?" He raised his voice, causing a majority of the students in the class to stare at us.

I looked down at my lap, avoiding his scrutinizing gaze. "I had a lot of fun last night," now it was my turn to be sarcastic.

He quickly stood up from his seat and pulled me with him. He pulled the top of my hoodie over my head so it was covering more than half of my face and placed his hand over my shoulder as he led me out of the classroom. I didn't know where he was taking me, but I followed him because I trusted him. He wasn't taking me to the nurse's office or to see any teacher. My bet was on an empty classroom or somewhere private where we could talk with no interruptions or people eavesdropping. Luckily, we were seniors in high school, so no student had the guts to question what was going on or say anything to any teacher. Even if the teachers saw us, they couldn't do anything because this was a private school, one of the most expensive private schools in the country, so you dared not touch any student.

Adrian and I had been best friends since Junior Secondary School Three (JSS3). Because of my abuse at home, I didn't bother to have friends because I didn't trust anyone, but Adrian refused to stay away from me and forced his way into my life. Looking back, I was grateful for his persistence. I didn't tell him the complete story, deliberately leaving out the part that I was being sexually abused.

He always encouraged me to report to the right authorities, but I couldn't out of fear. Not only fear for my stepfather but also my mother: I didn't know how she was going to react to the news. Though Adrian was a guy and I had no initial reason to trust him, he had somehow won my trust; call it instincts.

Adrian finally came to a halt and so did I. He touched the edges of my hood, silently asking me for permission, and I nodded. A gasp left his lips when he could fully see my face. He cupped my cheeks, forcing me to meet his gaze.

"Funke," he breathed. "What happened?"

I fought the tears from slipping as I looked into his eyes. It was hard to speak because it felt like I was in a chokehold, and that brought memories of my stepfather's sexual abuse: how he would pin me to the wall, the couch, the bed and wrap his large fingers around my neck, putting pressure enough to have me gasping for air and my face to redden then he'd roughly push himself inside me, his pace too fast that it would all become a blur to me. Sometimes I'd pass out from the pressure or sometimes I'd beg him to let me go, which he never did. On the days I was silent, he'd hit me and yell at me to plead for mercy, to plead to be free from him. Like a puppet on a string, I had to obey. It always felt like the walls of our house were too thick for anyone on the outside to hear my cries.

And like that, I let the tears slip from my eyes. Adrian was quick to pull me to his chest, offering all the comfort I needed. I didn't move, accepting the comfort he offered. It was nice to know that there was someone out there who cared for my well-being.

I sniffled and found the strength to pull from Adrian's hold, then I wiped my eyes and looked at him. I figured it was time to tell him the rest of the story. I opened my mouth to speak, only to close it again. Like a fish out of water, I kept opening and closing my mouth, but no words left my lips.

Adrian patted me on the back, encouraging me in his way. I took in a deep breath and let it out before opening my mouth once again and this time words left them, but not words I had originally planned.

"I tried to run away last night, but he caught me and beat me up. He forced me to sleep under his bed all night and- and…"

"Oh Lord," Adrian once again pulled me to him, cradling me in his arms and telling me it was going to be okay.

Despite my trust in Adrian, I refused to believe the words that left his lips. It would not be okay, not until I left that house, and even when I would, the images and horrible memories would forever haunt me.

Adrian pulled away, but he still slightly pressed my body to his. "Why can't you just report to the authorities? There will surely be people out there who can help you, organizations, and law firms. Let them sue that bastard and make him pay for what he is doing to you." He suggested once again, but I wasn't having it.

I pushed him, "no, no, I can't do that!" I pulled my hood over my head. "Even death is not a suitable punishment for that man," I said with anger before I took off down the flight of stairs.

"Funke, wait!" Adrian yelled after me, but I refused to stop.

I was an athlete, a very good one at that, but Adrian was one too, so it did not shock me when he caught up with me. As I was about to push open the bathroom door, he was in front of me, stopping me from going in.

"Look, I'm sorry. I can't just sit down and watch you suffer like this." He held both my shoulders and slightly bent forward so he could look me in the eye even though I had my hood on.

I sighed, "I'll think about it Adrian, but right now, can you at least let me use the bathroom?" I shrugged his hands off of me.

He stepped away from the door. "I'll be here."

I sent a swift nod his way before walking into the bathroom. Like I said earlier, this was one of the most expensive private schools in Nigeria, so we had to see the works of our money. This bathroom was only for the Senior Secondary School Three (SSS3) students. Though all the bathrooms in the school had a similar fashion: the mirror, paper towel, hand wash dispenser, and a crazy tap, this one was the cleanest and was way bigger than the rest.

37

This school had four restrooms for the students and three for the teachers and administrators. They treated the SSS3 students like kings and queens, which was why we had a separate restroom for us.

I took off my hood and looked at myself, or rather, the person I had become in the mirror. A bruise had formed on my left cheek and no amount of concealer could hide it. It had swollen so badly. I had a cut on the left side of my upper lip and another cut on my right eyebrow. My eyes had lost the brightness in them, which made me look like a zombie. They were never that bright because of all the heavy emotions I carried with me, but this time around they were duller than the usual dull. My grey eye was almost light brown, and my brown eye could be mistaken for black. My hair, which was usually packed up or styled in some sort of way, was in a tangled mess. I was sure my mother would be disappointed if she saw my hair this way.

Though she never paid much attention to other parts of my body or aspects of my life, she paid attention to my hair. She always made sure that my hair was trim and proper at all times. I had been growing my hair right from birth and never for one day had I cut it. I didn't object because my mother wanted it that way. My stepfather always enjoyed pulling at my hair during any of his awful sessions. My scalp always felt like it was on fire because of the constant tugging.

I reached for the elastic band in the pocket of my hoodie and quickly packed my hair up in what I liked to call an afro ponytail. This morning, I was too sad to pay any attention to my hair.

I splashed water on my face to wash off the tears that had dried up, then I reached for the paper towels and dabbed my face dry. I looked at my reflection in the mirror, satisfied with the damage control I had done.

This should do. I thought to myself.

I pulled up my hood and walked out of the bathroom.

True to his words, Adrian was standing by the door, waiting for me. When he heard the door open, he looked up at me and shook his head sympathetically.

"Come on," he took me by my hand and led us out of that area.

"Where are you taking me?" I asked when we walked past our classroom.

"To the nurse's office," he told me. "Don't worry, you don't even have to go in. I'm getting the drug for you."

Like before, I didn't protest, and I let him drag me to the nurse's office, which was not in the same block as our classrooms. It was in another building directly opposite our classrooms, but there was a fair distance between them.

When we got to the nurse's office Adrian went in and came out a few minutes after with two tablets of *Paracetamol* and a bottle of water. I took the tablets and nearly finished the bottle of water.

Adrian studied me. "Are you okay?"

"Yeah, thanks," I nodded, smiling stiffly at him to show my gratitude.

I would have taken painkillers at home, but my stepfather hid all the ones in the house, so I either had to suffer in pain or find one out of the house.

Adrian walked away, and I followed him. He reached out to hold my hand and squeezed it lightly as a sign of encouragement. As we walked back to our class, I couldn't help but wonder when all this was going to end.

Chicago

Chapter Four

It all ended faster than I ever imagined and I am happier now and proud of myself for adding one more person to my short list of friends. The journey to this point was far from smooth, but it was worth it.

Lucinda is a co-worker and now my friend. We hit it off pretty fast and Adrian is jealous because of that. I am taller than her by a few inches, but she's a brunette with the prettiest blue eyes I have ever seen. She is talkative, but I don't mind; I find it hard to zone out when she has the ball in her court, which is good because that seems to happen with everyone, Adrian partially included. She isn't aware of my life issues and I have no plans to tell her since we're probably never going to see each other again after the summer break. She lives in Los Angeles and only came over to spend some time with her cousins who live here. Even if we never see each other after this and we never communicate again, she's someone I will never forget.

The other person I'm tolerating is Miss McClain, the owner of the store and my mother's friend and that is the reason she hired me and Adrian. She is in her mid-thirties and a single mother, just like my mum. I think that is one thing that bonds them. She runs this little clothing store, which appears to be enough to keep her and her daughter going, but I do believe she has other small businesses she's running. I've never met her daughter because, just like me, she's on a vacation out of the country.

"Funke, out front," Lucy calls out to me from the break room.

I look around the store for Adrian's familiar lock of brown hair because I can't leave the counter unattended. Lucy called me to attend to a customer who walked in when she could do it herself. I wonder what she is doing in the break room when it isn't time for her break yet. It isn't until the next thirty minutes.

Adrian emerges from the rack of clothes, two unfamiliar guys behind him. One is blonde while the other has black hair; they both are tall and slim. Adrian places the clothes in his hand on the counter and I immediately get to work. When I'm done, I neatly but roughly fold the clothes in a bag and push them forward.

"$50," I announce, looking up at the two guys. The one with the black hair hands me his card and in a minute I complete the transaction. "Thank you for shopping with us," I say automatically as I watch the guys walk out of the store.

Adrian moves from in front of the counter to where I am standing behind it. "So I was wondering if you want to go see a movie with me today after work?" He asks nervously, his fingers twitching. I want to decline his offer at first, but I quickly change my mind. I am tired of staying at home and doing nothing but watching TV all afternoon. Maybe I should bring some change into my life. Adrian and I have gone out a few times, not by my will, so I might as well just agree this time around.

"Alright," I smile.

Adrian visibly relaxes. "I thought you would decline my offer."

I chuckle. "I'm full of surprises."

"Oh, thank goodness you guys are here," Miss McClain, the owner of the shop, joins us from the door behind us. "I need you guys to cover two extra hours." She claps her hands, giving us a tight smile.

I look at Adrian and his face drops. "What about Kelly and Jack?"

"They won't be able to make it from their road trip on time. They are stuck in some kind of traffic," Miss McClain answers, still giving us a sad smile.

Adrian groans and so do I. Kelly and Jack are coworkers here, but they make it their life mission to cause us problems. I'm so glad that we didn't get the same shift with them. They are to take over from us when we walk out of here at the end of our shift and close the store by seven pm.

"Who goes on a road trip during the week?" I shake my head.

"I'll double your pay for the week," Miss McClain beams, still trying to get us to agree.

"Fine," Adrian groans and walks to the back office, where Ms. McClain came out from.

SAVING HER

She looks at me and I shrug, "alright." This means no movie later on.

"Thank you so much." She tries to touch me, but I move away before she can and she awkwardly drops her hands and disappears behind the door she came out from. I don't like human contact, especially if I barely know you and I barely know this woman, but I have to tolerate her to keep my job.

I turn back around to face the store as I bring my head back into the game of work.

Chicago

Chapter Five

"Since we can no longer go to the movies, what do you want to do tonight?" Adrian asks me as we walk side by side on the busy streets.

We just got off from work, thirty minutes later than Miss McClain had told us we would. Kelly and Jack were very late. I am exhausted from sitting down on that stool for long hours, waiting for a customer to walk up to me and purchase something.

"We do the usual, go home, eat, Netflix, and sleep," I shrug. I'm not too happy with the turn of events, but we have to live with it.

"Don't you get bored doing that? That's all we do when we get back from work," Adrian exclaims, and I gasp.

SAVING HER

"Point of correction. That is all *I* do. Most of the time you're at a party and you get back home by almost midnight and yes, I enjoy it!" I yell and storm away from him, careful not to bump into people on the way.

I hear him yelling my name, but I don't stop. The store is very close to the house so we are almost home. I can see the house from where I am. I know Adrian is trying to look out for me and help me have the best time during this vacation, but it's not that easy for me. Human interaction is my weakness and I suck at it. Plus, we still have ten months to go; this is a one-year vacation.

Now on our front porch, I struggle to get my key out of my bag, and as I am about to pull it out, Adrian holds my hands and stops me. He is breathing heavily, obviously from trying to catch up with me.

"Look Funke, I'm sorry–"

I pull my hand from his grip and that silences him. After I take out my keys, unlock the door and get in, I slam the door shut in his face. I hear him groan from behind the door before he opens it.

He wraps his hands around me and pulls me to his chest. I don't struggle from his grip, but hug him back. I am pissed at him, but I still understand him and where he is coming from. Maybe I need to go out more and meet people my age. That should help me.

"I'm sorry Funke, I am," he apologizes again.

"It's fine, I understand," I nod, and he pulls me even closer to him.

When we pull away from the hug, he clears his throat. "I'll be going to a party around seven and I just thought you should know." He tells me as he takes off his shoes.

I take off my shoes too. "Can I go with you?"

His eyes widen. "You want to go to a party with me?" He asks in disbelief.

I am shocked at myself too, "yes." I nod.

"That is great. Trust me, we're going to have so much fun," he hugs me once again and dramatically places a kiss on my forehead.

Lagos

Chapter Six

I heard my name and I looked up. I dropped the pen I was doodling with and zoned back into reality.

"Yes?" I looked at the teacher that was now in front of me instead of right by the board where she usually was. It surprised me she was speaking directly to me. People hardly did that: they preferred to speak to Adrian, who would then relay the information to me.

"I said you would do your project with Mide," she repeated and I robotically nodded my head, hoping she would walk away already.

"And what is the project?" The very young literature teacher folded her arms as if to say she was ready for me.

Quickly scanning through my head, I remembered what she said at the beginning of the class. "Write a review on Castle of Otranto," I answered, and with a nod, she walked away without another word and I got ready to zone out again.

Being a loner and seen as the freak had its perks that I enjoyed. One was that no one disturbed me, not even the teachers. In the beginning, everyone kept trying to make me talk, to engage me with the class activities, but all their silly attempts were futile. With time, they gave up, especially when my grades never dropped.

If you were not Adrian, then don't talk to me. Some students of the class still had their eyes on me and, feeling bold, I maintained eye contact with one of them. I think he was the Mide the teacher wanted me to work with. His funeral because I was the worst person to work with.

I didn't look away, and neither did Mide, until his friend nudged his side and he finally looked away. I went back to my doodling as my mind drifted off to my imagination again.

At the end of the class, I put my books away, ready to rest my head on the desk, when I heard my name again.

I groaned. "Who the fuck is that?"

SAVING HER

"The principal wants to see you." A voice that belonged to one of my classmates said. I didn't know who it was.

I slowly stood up, feeling the eyes of Adrian and every other person in the class on me. I ignored them as usual. The classroom was almost empty because most students had gone downstairs for Inter-House sports practice after the bell had rung. I successfully ignored the secretary when I got to the principal's office and knocked on the door.

"Come in," I heard her voice, not loud but firm.

"Funke, please take a seat." She adjusted her glasses on the bridge of her nose as she looked up from some papers in front of her.

"Good morning ma," I greeted as I sat down.

"How are you today?" She asked, as if she cared.

"Fine." I stared blankly at her.

"Your house mistress, Mrs. Balogun, spoke to me about your unwillingness to take part in the inter-house sports activities." She stopped talking as if waiting for me to speak. I kept shut and watched her.

She sighed when I remained silent. "I know you are always calm and reserved, but sometimes you need to come out, be involved." She paused again. This time I nodded, and that made her sigh in relief. "Now please go join your housemates for practice. If you have any issues, just let me know." She offered me a smile, and I gave her a stiff one in return.

As I walked out of the office, I met Adrian, who was standing on the opposite wall, arms folded. He looked up when I stepped out. It was obvious what the principal had called me for.

"Don't." I gave him a warning look.

He smiled and raised his hands in mock surrender. "I said nothing."

I walked ahead of him and he fell in step with me, so we were walking side by side. "You were about to."

He laughed. "Come on." He took my hand and led me to a part of the school's field where students huddled up and were talking.

Silence ensued as we stepped into their midst. People talked about me as usual and I paid them no mind. I was guessing these were the *White house* members.

SAVING HER

Not that I cared so much about the event, but I was happy when I found out that Adrian and I picked the same house. Before Adrian and I became friends during the first two years of junior school, I took part in these events and I had discovered my skill for running, pretty fast might I add. With time when I started pulling more to myself and ignoring everybody, I stopped running and slowly people stopped asking me to come run for the house or to join the school's athletic team. I never engaged in anything concerning social gatherings and my mother never asked why, so I didn't bother myself.

In case you were wondering what *Inter-house sport* is, it's when schools divide the students into groups and call those groups houses, named after colors or persons or things, but every house has its color assigned to them. These houses simply competed in sports activities. It's an extra-curricular activity which should to be fun. Well, it is fun, but I refused to cooperate.

"This must be a dream." The voice of the house mistress pulled me out of my thoughts. "What did I miss?" She looked between me and Adrian, the surprise on her face not hidden: the surprise to see me there.

"It was the principal, not me," Adrian simply answered and tucked his hands into the pocket of his sports shorts, shifting his weight from one foot to the other.

"Well, we're happy you're here. God knows we need more athletes." She said before clapping her hands.

"Not everyone," I heard a very familiar voice from beside me and I looked her way. It was none other than Jasmine Adekola.

She hated me for reasons unknown to me. No one spoke to me and even if they did, they didn't do it with so much hate as she did. Every chance she got, she gave me a nasty look, but I didn't care.

I heard she and Adrian were the house captains and from the whispers here and there; she liked Adrian, but he didn't fancy her. They had a fling once at the beginning of SS2 but it only lasted for a short while because Adrian didn't like how she always spoke to me, and according to him, he couldn't fuck someone who hated his best friend. That only made her harsh words worse.

I ignored her and focused on the house mistress, who was saying something about the march-past. Some group of students left us, leaving only a few of us behind.

"So, let's see how fast you've gotten Funke." Mrs. Balogun said and everyone turned to me.

I shook my head.

"Come on," Adrian placed an arm over my shoulder

I looked at everyone's faces and only a few were familiar.

"Fine," I gave in.

"Great! Jasmine, Funke, Simi and Chioma let's see." Mrs. Balogun said and everyone dispersed.

"Come on," Adrian led me to the tracks where Jasmine and two other girls I didn't know stood. Mrs. Balogun stood beside Jasmine and I made my way over to the other side, beside the girl I think was Chioma.

Adrian sent me a wink, causing me to roll my eyes.

"On your mark," Mrs. Balogun called, and all three girls got on one knee.

I reluctantly followed them.

"Set!" they all shifted, so they were all bent over with the tips of their fingers pressed to the ground.

I copied them again, this time seconds slower.

"Go!" she finally called, and we all took off, well they did more than me. I was barely using any speed; you could say I was jogging.

As I ran past Adrian, I knew he said a full sentence, but all I heard was "for me."

With a sigh, I picked up my speed, and I met up with the girls ahead. The first person I passed was Chioma, then Simi. As I got to Jasmine, she ran in front of me, causing me to slow down as we passed the finish line.

I halted and unlike the others, who bent over to catch their breath; I stood with my hands on my waist. Jasmine looked at me and she smirked. I rolled my eyes and looked away. Adrian was making his way over to me with a huge grin on his face.

"Why are you grinning?" I asked him.

"You dusted them. I can imagine if you ran at that much speed from the beginning." He shook my shoulders, and I pushed his hand away.

We all walked back to where we started from and Mrs. Balogun had a huge smile on her face.

SAVING HER

"You're going to have to do that again and this time, I want you to start with that kind of speed." She directed the last part to me. "Guys, let's see what you have."

I made my way to the bleachers and sat down as I watched not only my house, but other houses run around the tracks and field.

This school had one thing that they were most proud of: the sports activities and facilities. We had the standard football pitch with the tracks surrounding it, not as big as stadiums but big enough for a high school, and the bleachers could hold over a hundred guests or two hundred, not sure. There was a lawn tennis court and a volleyball court and unlike other schools, they were separate and not made as one. Then there was the indoor basketball court popularly known as the gym and the indoor swimming pool, everything Olympic standard but just big enough for a high school. Everything in the school reminded me of high schools in American movies. The only difference was that there were no lockers in the hallways. They joined our lockers with our desks in the classroom, but we had a locker room close to the gym. Athletes used it more or during times like this when we were preparing for Inter-house sports.

I was called to run again, and I did. This time I sped up at the beginning and slowed down close to the finish line when I realized I had left a vast gap between me and the other girls. I also noticed that everyone around watched the race and even when we were done for the day, people still looked at me and talked amongst themselves.

Since the practice was scheduled for the last of the school hours, most students that weren't running or involved in one sports event or the other left almost immediately after the last bell of the day. So now we were only a few people in the locker room. I waited until most girls had showered and changed before I got into the shower.

Though I never used the locker room but every other week, I made sure I had some extra clothes in my locker in case I ever needed to change. Most of the time it was the school's official sweatpants and T-shirt that were also allowed, especially at a time as this or when we needed an emergency change of clothes. Every student had them.

I quickly showered and changed and by the time I was done, I was the last person left, or so I thought. Jasmine came out of nowhere and stood in my way.

"What do you want?" I slung my bag over my shoulder, not having the strength for her.

"What do *you* want? First Adrian, and now you want to outshine me on the tracks, not happening." She shook her head.

I sighed, already angered. I wanted to say something, but decided against it, knowing that she wasn't worth my breath.

"I don't have the time for bullshit." I pushed past her and ignored her as she spewed insults at me, words that I'd heard many times over.

I found Adrian by his car where he usually was on the days when we didn't walk out of the school building together. He looked up from his phone when I was in front of him, "what took you so long?" He unlocked the door and opened the passenger's door for me and closed it when I sat comfortably.

As he got into the car, I told him what happened and he told me to ignore her as he drove me home.

"Why are you just getting home?" I heard his voice, even though I had my earphones on as I stepped into the house.

"I had practice," I answered as I pulled one earphone out, not bothering to pause the music.

"What practice?" His questions were pissing me off, as always.

"Inter-house sports practice, I'm running." I was at the foot of the stairs now and I looked up at my stepfather, who was at the top of the stairs.

"Whatever. Just cook for me. I'm hungry."

I closed my eyes for a second and inhaled. "Yes sir," I breathed.

Lagos

Chapter Seven

"Funke get down here!" My stepfather yelled from downstairs making me groan in frustration.

What does he want this time around?

I reluctantly got up from the bed and walked out of my room, making sure to leave the door slightly open in case I needed to run back in anytime soon. After a long while of having no door or curtain to give me some privacy, my stepfather got tired of it so he gave me my door back.

I ran my hands on the walls as I ran down the stairs, my stepfather didn't like being kept waiting, and I had learned that the hard way. The closer I got to the living room the more convinced I was that I was going crazy. My mother's laughter reverberated through the house and that made me quicken my step.

Lo and behold there she was, laughing like she had no care in the world. When she saw me, her eyes lit up and she smiled at me. "Surprise!" She opened her arms ushering a hug.

"Mum," I said unable to hide the shock in my voice. "What are you doing here?" I accepted her embrace.

"I came to surprise you for your birthday. Happy birthday in advance dear," she smiled so widely that I was scared that her mouth was going to split rather quickly.

"My birthday?" I asked getting confused. "What is today's date?"

My mum gasped, "Don't tell me you don't remember your birthday." She turned to look at my stepfather as if he could give her the answer she needed. My stepfather just shrugged as if it was not his business. Well, it wasn't.

My mum looked back and forth between her husband and me and she cupped my face in her hands, "dear, today is February nine, and tomorrow being the tenth is your birthday." She dropped her hands to my shoulders, "and we are going to have a party here tomorrow night to celebrate, it's your big eighteen!" She shook me slightly and that helped me properly arrange my thoughts.

I would be eighteen meaning I could now be free from this horrible life I was living. I could run away to somewhere with the little cash I had been saving for so long, start a new life, get a menial job and be happy for the first time in years.

I know you must wonder why I was this old—according to Nigerian standards—and still in high school, well the answer was simple: My mum and her family who were living in America moved to Nigeria but she raped barely a month after arriving and so she had me. Before I came into this world, both her parents died, leaving her family with little to nothing. After I was born, she moved away from her family and got a menial job that paid little to nothing. With time, she pulled through and she employed her art skills and started a small interior decorating business that had grown so much now. Having me was an immense blow on her, so I only started school when she could comfortably afford it, which was when I was four years old.

"A party?" I asked her getting confused again.

"Yes a party, you can invite your friends, classmates, you know." She sounded way more excited about it than I was.

"A party, mum I don't have friends," I pointed out, dropping my head.

Her slim finger raised my chin, "but you have classmates and church members who would be more than happy to attend, don't worry about the numbers, and just get ready to have fun." She winked, "now," she draped her hand over my shoulder as she directed me to the front door, "we need to go shopping for a dress, you have to look your best tomorrow night." She grabbed her handbag that was seated just beside her husband. "See you later hun," she blew him a kiss as she dragged me out of the house with her.

I didn't think I was ready for this but I was willing to give it a try. I had read books and watched movies about people who went shopping with their mothers and how much fun they had, I hoped I could get to experience it too, I hoped.

SAVING HER

"You can start making calls to invite whoever you want to invite and I'll invite my people too, I have friends who have kids your age," my mum said ushering me to pick up my phone, but it felt like her words had an underlying meaning.

I shrugged and picked up my phone from the table we sat at. After walking around *Ikeja City Mall* looking for the perfect dress, we finally found one and by then we were exhausted, so we had an ice cream break. I got the ice cream, and she got a soda.

I had never really gone shopping before, only when my mum sent money to get some new clothes or stuff that I needed for myself which Ayanda, our housekeeper or *personal nanny* as my mum called her, couldn't get for me did I go shopping. I'd only gone shopping with Adrian once and that was when he begged me to come with him.

I sent a message to my class group chat inviting them to the party, not failing to add my address to the message. Many people replied almost immediately, saying they would be there. My phone started ringing and Adrian's name popped up on the screen.

I smiled at my mum before sliding my finger across the screen to answer the call, "hey."

"Party at your house? Tomorrow?" Adrian was confused, as expected.

"Yep, surprise!" I faked my surprised tone, and I knew he could read through it. I sighed, "alright, my mum just arrived and said she's throwing me a birthday party tomorrow. You're coming, right?"

"Of course, I'm coming. I just had to be sure that it was you." He chuckled, "I have to go now. I'll call you later." He hung up.

"And you said you don't have friends." My mum rolled her eyes at me like a teenager.

I rolled my eyes too, "at least half of my classmates are coming."

She clapped her hands like an excited teenage girl who had just seen her favorite artist. "That's great, oh I can't wait for tomorrow." She stood up, clearing the table.

I stood up too, helping her to clear the table, "mum I'm still trying to figure out if this is my birthday or yours,"

She laughed, "I'm just excited for you, that's all." We got rid of my empty cup and her empty can of soda.

"My baby is growing so fast." She linked our hands as we both walked out of the eatery.

I tried not to think of the negative parts of her sentence as we made our way home.

Chapter Eight

I heard the door opening before the knock registered in my brain. I turned around to see who it was. My jaw dropped when I beheld the human before me.

He was wearing in black ripped jeans and a black button-up shirt with the top three buttons open. He gelled his hair to the back and for the first time; I saw him on a black small hoop earring that was on his left ear only. Long ago, I noticed he had his left ear pierced, but he never wore an earring.

Adrian stepped into the room, a small smirk on his face as he drank me in from head to toe.

"You look beautiful," he said as he snaked an arm around my waist and pulled me to his chest for a hug.

On a normal day when we hugged, my face always rested on his chest. This time around, I was resting my head on his shoulder because of my heels.

I hugged him back, draping my arm around his neck. "And you look," I paused for dramatic effect. "Hot."

We pulled away from the hug, and I could swear I saw his cheeks tint pink. He cleared his throat before digging his hand into his pocket and taking out a small black box, then he handed the box to me. "Happy birthday."

I smiled, "thank you."

I opened the box and once again my jaw dropped. In the box was a silver necklace with a small scarlet crystal as the pendant. I smiled wider and looked up at him.

It wasn't the necklace that gave me this much joy, but the thought behind it. Giving someone a scarlet crystal meant you were giving them strength, vitality, willpower, and dedication and as if he could read my mind he was giving me exactly what I needed.

"Thank you," I threw myself on him, pulling him into a bear hug.

He was stiff for a second before he hugged me back, wrapping his arms around me. I could smell his cologne more now. In all honesty, it was a delightful scent and I could stay there forever.

He pulled away from the hug and took the necklace from the box, then turned me around. I moved my hair out of the way so he could clip the necklace on for me. When he was done, he pushed me to stand in front of the mirror just where I was standing before he walked into the room.

The necklace was a perfect fit with my dress, which was a black and red sequin body con dress with a plunging V-neck that stopped mid-thigh. The sequin part was black and the lower part which was red hugged my body in the right places.

My skin never entertained very visible scars, so whatever scar was on my skin was hardly noticeable. I also used a body lotion and a body wash that did the job of keeping my skin fresh and smooth, but some scars just couldn't go away like a few on my middle back.

I sighed with contentment. I was keeping this forever.

Chicago

Chapter Nine

My hands play with the scarlet pendant on my neck as Lucy dolls me up for the party. After I told Adrian that I would go to the party with him, he called Lucy to help me get ready for the party. Adrian knows I can handle my own, since this isn't the first party that I am getting ready for, but I don't mind the help. Lucy is a great company.

When Lucy found out this is the first party I am going to in Chicago, she started talking about how the parties here are: the dos and the don'ts. She sounded way more excited about the party than I am. I mean, what's the big deal about a party? I asked her to come with me but she said that she has a babysitting job to get to after she leaves here, but she will surely make it to the next one.

"All done," she exclaims as she stands up straighter.

"Can I see myself now?" She refused to let me look in the mirror as she worked on my face and my hair.

She nods, "go wear your dress." She tosses the dress at me and pushes me to the bathroom to get changed.

I oblige, closing the bathroom door behind me. I strip off my shorts and shirt and wear the gown. It is a handless black dress with a deep back cut that stops mid-thigh and exposes my cleavage.

I look in the mirror and someone who I can't recognize is staring back at me. The makeup is subtle just as I want it, and it highlights my difference in eye colors. My hair is down in a low afro ponytail and it pools in its curly glory on my back. Beautiful is the first word that crosses my mind just looking at myself.

"You're not staying in there forever, are you?" Lucy says from behind the door, pulling me from my self-admiration.

I open the door and Lucy's jaw drops when she sees me. "What do you think?" I twirl.

"You look amazing," she grins. "Adrian won't be able to resist you tonight," she winks.

"Oh please, Adrian doesn't like me that way," I wave her off and move to get my sandals from my wardrobe.

"What do you mean, that guy likes you *that* way and I'm sure you feel the same way about him too," she nudges my shoulder.

I sigh and sit on the bed to wear my sandals. "Even if he does and I do like him, he doesn't want a relationship and I will not force him into something he isn't interested in."

"How do you know he doesn't want a relationship?" She sits down beside me.

I take in a deep breath, then let it out. I don't want to snap at Lucy. She has done nothing to make me do it. She's just being a little too curious.

"Just drop it, Lucy," I say instead and she immediately gets the message, and she doesn't speak about it again.

I finish buckling the second leg of my sandal and stand up. "I think I'm ready."

A knock sounds on my door and Lucy stands up to open it. I hear Adrian's voice, "Is she rea–" he stops mid-sentence when his eyes land on me.

"Hi," I smile.

"Hi you look amazing," he says and stretches his hand out to me.

I place my hand in his and let him pull me to him. "You don't look so bad either." I tell him.

He is wearing blue jeans and a white shirt. His hair is messy but a sexy kind of mess and he has on his black loop earring, which is the same one he wore for my birthday party instead of the silver one he has been wearing since. I think the black one is his favorite.

Lucy winks at me as we walk past her and make our way downstairs. Adrian's hand feels warm against mine and it helps calm my nerves.

I hope I don't regret tonight.

"If you need me, I'm only one call away," Lucy says as we all step out of the house.

Adrian locks the door and puts the key in his pocket. We walk to his car and Lucy walks to hers parked just behind Adrian's. Since Adrian is an American citizen, he has his driver's license, so he is driving us to the party, meaning he will not drink tonight. Works for me.

I wave Lucy goodbye and Adrian opens the door to the passenger's seat and I get in. Seconds after, he gets into the driver's seat and starts driving. He never drives us to work because of the short distance and the fact that I like the walk, so he only uses the car when going to other places.

I reach out to switch on the radio at the same time that he does, making our hands touch. He is the first to pull away, clearing his throat. This thing between us, which I believe is nothing, is driving me crazy. I shake the thoughts from my head and push the radio button.

Secret Love Song by *Little Mix* comes on and this time around, I'm the one to clear my throat at the irony of the whole thing. I believe some things are best swept under the rug and never to be spoken about. Adrian's actions clarified that things between us are better off left the way they are.

The drive to the party isn't short, and neither is it long. "We're here," Adrian announces as he parks his car behind another.

There are cars parked on both sides of the street and we can hear the music from the party, which is two houses down from where we are standing. I can feel the vibrations of the bass shaking up my entire being.

"What time did you say the party was supposed to start?" I ask as we walk down the street.

"By eight, why?" Adrian's eyes land on me.

"What time is it?" I gesture to the watch on his wrist.

He lifts his wrist, adjusting the head of the watch to his line of vision. "Fifteen past eight."

"Wow, and the party is already in full swing," I shake my head at the ridiculousness of it. Americans do party hard.

"Welcome to America," he chuckles and takes my hand in his as we head straight for the front door.

There are many people on the front porch and littering the lawn, so I am not surprised at how full the house is. Adrian pulls me through the crowd of people covered in sweat and up the stairs. I'm clueless about where he's taking me, but I trust him.

He stops walking in front of a white door and knocks before opening the door and walking in with me behind him. Why knock when you're going to open the door without waiting for a response?

This room is less occupied, unlike downstairs. There are only four people in here: A brunette guy is sitting on a chair by a desk, a blonde and two guys with black hair are sitting on the bed. They all have intimidating looks, mainly because of their visible tattoos, all except for the blonde, who looks like the innocent one.

"Adrian, you made it," the brunette says when they notice us walk into the room.

"Of course," Adrian walks towards him and they do the bro hug thing while I just stand there awkwardly.

"Guys, this is Funke, my best friend. Funke this is Aiden," he points to the brunette, "Dakota," the blonde, "Derek and Josh." He points to the guys with black hair. The one who has fewer tattoos and looks less intimidating is Derek, and the other is Josh.

"Hi," I say awkwardly as I shift from one foot to the other. I always get super uncomfortable when I'm around guys, but because Adrian is here, my nerves aren't spiraling out of control.

"These are my friends. I've known Aiden and Dakota since childhood," Adrian explains, and I nod as it all comes back to me.

He once talked about some friends he had when he lived in Chicago before he moved to Nigeria. He never mentioned them more than twice, so I never brought them up. Adrian moved to Nigeria when he was five, so I could imagine how he felt meeting the people he had had an early childhood with again after so many years. I can describe all five of them in this room with one word: hot.

"Nice to meet you, Funke. Adrian talks about you a lot," Aiden says with a small smile on his lips, stretching his hand out to shake mine.

I cringe at how he calls my name, but I brush it off. It's not his fault. "Nice to meet you too," I shake his hand and I mentally pat myself on the back for not freaking out.

"Has he taken a–" Dakota says, but Adrian shushes him.

I look at both of them, confused about what is going on. What was Derek about to ask me?

"Nice to meet you," Dakota says, this time around, and my shoulders drop. I want to know what he wanted to ask me.

I exchange pleasantries with the other guys, and they all seem nice despite their intimidating looks.

SAVING HER

"Come on, let's go to the basement. The actual party is down there," Derek says as he walks out of the room.

Adrian and I are the last to leave the room, so Adrian locks the door behind him. We weave our way through the crowd of drunken teenagers and when we finally get to the basement; I heave a sigh of relief. There are people in the basement, but not as many as those upstairs. I can at least breathe properly here.

We all sit down on the couches that are huddled up in one corner in a circle. Adrian and I sit on one, Aiden and Dakota sit on the one opposite us while Derek and Josh sit on the one beside Adrian. To me, Derek and Josh seem to be the quiet ones in this little group, or maybe they aren't part of this group.

"You want a drink?" Dakota asks us as he takes a swig from the cup he filled on our way down here.

I shake my head and so does Adrian.

"Why?" Derek asks.

"I don't drink," I answer. I never really liked alcohol, so I never saw a reason to drink.

"I'm driving," Adrian answers.

"Get an Uber. You're drinking, you too," Derek points to me and stands up, headed to the coolers.

"It's your first party in America, so you need to drink; just one." Aiden raises his finger to emphasize his point.

"Whatever guys," Adrian rolls his eyes, obviously giving up on if he should drink.

"So, how do you like America so far?" Derek reappears and hands Adrian and me a cup each, filled with a cold liquid.

I mutter a thank you and hold the cup with both hands, enjoying the feel of the cold from the cup. "America is okay, I guess," I answer Derek's question.

I take a sip of my drink and cringe as it slides down my throat. The initial taste isn't pleasant, and it burns before the real taste finally melts on my tongue.

I hear Dakota chuckle, "it's Vodka, mixed of course." He answers the question floating in my head..

"Well, it is one hell of a drink," one large sip after the other, and I slowly fall into numbness.

Lagos

Chapter Ten

My mother's impatient voice pulled both of us away from our thoughts before we made our way out of my room. We met my mum on the stairs and she gave a half-smile to Adrian. I knew what that smile meant: *what the hell are you doing up here?*

I gave her a half-smile too as I pushed Adrian down the stairs with me, in a rush to get away from her scrutinizing eyes and her questions that were yet to come.

They transformed our living room to a dance floor. The couches and chairs shifted to the corners to create enough space to dance in the middle. They had made the bar, which only my stepfather used bigger to accommodate more people sitting there. Someone was behind the bar, serving drinks, non-alcoholic drinks, I supposed.

At my appearance in the room, everyone turned to look at me and started cheering. People I knew from school and church, together with people I didn't know, were there. It didn't matter to me who came and who didn't. All that mattered was that Adrian was here, and I wasn't alone, even though people surrounded me.

They all started singing the *Happy Birthday* song to me and Adrian unhooked our arms and stood in front of me, joining them to sing. The crowd made a path for someone to pass through. My mother's radiant face was the first thing I saw before my eyes landed on the massive cake in her hands. Someone came from behind her, holding another cake, then handed the cake to Adrian.

Both cakes had lit candles on them, ready for me to blow the flames out after I made a wish. I never believed in making wishes and having them come true because all my life, I'd been making wishes that never came true, but for today, I was going to believe that wishes came true and blow those candles out.

They all stopped singing and my mother said, "make a wish dear."

SAVING HER

I looked around me, then closed my eyes, knowing exactly what to wish for. *I wish this trauma was over.* Then I blew the candles out on both cakes.

Everyone in the room cheered once again as two people took the cakes from my mum and Adrian. My mum hugged me and the music picked up. Everyone started dancing and people came around to wish me a happy birthday. Adrian stayed by my side, rendering me the human support I needed, knowing my inexistent relationship with any other human but him and my dysfunctional family.

After they were done with their wishes, which I knew most weren't from their hearts, since a majority of them didn't know me on a personal level, Adrian dragged me to the dance floor. I wanted to resist at first, but so far; I was having fun, something that I never had the pleasure of truly experiencing before. Even if it was going to last for only one night, then I would gladly take it.

A new song came on and Adrian wrapped his hands around my hips. I flinched and completely distanced myself from him. When I agreed to dance, I didn't know that he was going to touch me like that. The only time the opposite

83

sex had held me like that was when my stepfather wanted to have his way with me and it was uncomfortable. I had to loosen up around Adrian for times like this, which may never happen again.

"Are you okay?" Adrian asked me, concerned.

"Yeah, I'm fine, sorry." I moved closer to him.

"You sure?" He slowly placed his hands around my hips once again, not sure how I was going to react. When he saw nothing was happening, he visibly relaxed.

"Yeah," I nodded and placed my hands on his shoulders.

I didn't know how to dance, so I just let my body move to the beat of the music and let Adrian guide me. It surprised me that my mum threw a party for me. Never in my wildest dreams would I have imagined something like this to happen.

My eyes scanned the room looking for her, but all I got were the faces of my classmates and church members and Adrian's face. His eyes were studying me closely. Our eyes met, and he looked away. The lights were not bright, but I could spot the blush that crept up his face. This was strange.

Since he was white, it was easy to spot a blush on his face. His hair, which was gelled perfectly, was now a bit out of place and in all honestly, he looked hotter than before.

Okay, something is wrong with me.

Our eyes met once again, and this time around, he didn't look away. I leaned toward him and spoke, "Why are you looking at me like that?"

"It's hard to take my eyes off of you Funke, you look so beautiful tonight, plus that dress is doing wonders on your body. You should dress up more often." He answered.

That's if my stepfather doesn't kill me. I wanted to say, but I decided it was best to keep shut. That way, I wouldn't say more than I intended.

Not only did the distance between our bodies shrink, our faces, too. His lips met mine, and he started kissing me. I didn't resist or try to stop him because my lips were moving with his and it clicked in that I was kissing Adrian, my very first kiss.

My arms went up to his hair and my fingers tangled it. I had wanted to do this for so long now. Running my hand through his hair was way better than I had imagined and dreamed about. Like we couldn't get close enough, he pulled me more to him and his hold on my waist tightened, but not in a way to hurt me. From my waist, his hands moved to my back and then cupped my face in one of his hands while the other remained on my back. My hands went lower, and I found them on his ripped chest.

All my dreams about Adrian were finally coming true: Him being my first kiss and getting to run my hands over his body and through his hair. Okay, maybe this was turning out to be a make-out session in public, but screw me, I was living my dreams.

Adrian pulled away, leaving us both gasping for air. His lips were swollen, and I was sure mine was no different. He leaned in and pecked my lips for a second.

"You wanna get out of here?" He nodded towards the kitchen.

I nodded. He intertwined our fingers before leading the way out of the living room. The chefs my mum hired were in the kitchen, running around. I noticed both of my cakes on the table, both untouched. The cake was going to be my treat for the night.

SAVING HER

Adrian had been at my house countless times, obviously when my stepfather wasn't at home, so he knew the way around the house both in and out. We walked past the pool and towards the other side where the guest house was. I used to hide out here whenever my stepfather's tortures were just too much for me to bear. A few times when Adrian came over and he couldn't find me inside the house, he would find me here, so this was like my haven. We sat on a beach chair that was on the balcony of the guest house, our bodies slightly turned towards each other and our knees almost touching.

"I hope you're having fun tonight?" He asked.

I looked at him, "well I am, thanks to you."

He smiled and I returned it. It felt so good to be smiling. I study his face and the way his eyes crinkled because of his smile. I smiled wider.

He reached out and took my hands in his. He brought my hands to his lips, softly kissing them, his lips lingering for more than a second. "I'm always here for you, you know that, right?" He still held my hands. I nodded in reply and he went on. "And for me to help you get through all you're going through, you need to tell me everything that is bothering you."

My heart sank with guilt at his words. I should have told him everything but I didn't and it made the guilt eat deeper into me. It wasn't like I didn't want to tell him, but every time I wanted to speak up, it became hard to breathe or talk like Seyi cursed me not to.

He noticed how my shoulders had slumped and my dampened mood, so he held my shoulders, making me straighten my back. "What's wrong?"

To Adrian, I was an open book, and he could read me without so much effort.

I took in a deep breath, mentally prepared to tell him, but my mother's voice stopped me short.

She was calling me in to cut my cake and open my gifts. "I think we should go," I told him as I stood up, now creating a gap between us. I would tell him some other time.

"What did you want to say?" He stood up and took hold of my hand.

I glanced at him before I turned around, taking the lead back into the house. "It's nothing."

He didn't reply, and I silently heaved a breath of relief. Maybe I wasn't ready to speak just yet.

When we got back inside, the music was at a lower volume and it looked like everyone was waiting for us, no it was me. Adrian followed me to where the cake was and stood beside me, urging me to cut the cake.

I took the knife and when I felt like it; I cut the cake.

Chicago

Chapter Eleven

I'm not one to cuddle up and get physically close to the opposite sex, so I'm shocked when I realize how close Adrian and I are standing. Yes, he is different in so many ways, but still a male. I shouldn't get too close to have my lips inches from his, but that is all I want to do right now and all my body desires to do. I blame the alcohol I've had too much of. Adrian, however, is in his right senses.

With Adrian, I have always wished to do things or done things I would never agree to do with another guy. I can't imagine myself kissing or making out with anyone but Adrian because it feels wrong.

The last time we kissed, we were both in our right senses and when we never talked about it, even when we had the chance, I felt my heart break in two. Though his words to me on our graduation day made me believe he has feelings for me but it is more than a year now and nothing from him still. Am I ready for another heartbreak? No, but I don't care as long as I get to kiss his lips again.

I press my lips to his, and my entire being gets submerged in a sea of ecstasy. His lips are just as I remember them: soft and it holds the power to set my entire being on fire. I feel my heart flutter and the zoo in my stomach wakes up. With his hands on my hips and mine around his neck, he pulls me closer to him, closing the gap between us. His body heat washes over me and I welcome it. Drunk or not, I am going to remember this moment. His hands slowly but roughly grab my ass and my hands sink deeper into his hair, tugging it. He groans and brushes my bottom lip with his tongue, asking for access, which I give him.

When his tongue is in my mouth, I feel my legs weaken and a moan escapes my lips. I push myself further into him so as not to lose my balance and he gets the memo, holding me tighter. My body aches for him and I want more.

I lose track of time while standing and making out, but I know that when we pull away, his hair is a mess and I am sure my lipstick is smudged. His eyes hold something that I have never seen before: lust. I move in to kiss him again, but he pulls away, making me furrow my eyebrows in confusion.

"Funke, I can't do this now," he closes his eyes for a second, taking his hands up to my waist and resting his forehead on mine.

"What do you mean?" My hand drops to his shoulders.

"You're drunk and I don't want you to regret anything in the morning," he takes his hands off me and my shoulders drop. This is not how I wanted this to play out.

"But… but you…" I distance myself from him, but I miss him almost instantly.

"No buts Funke, you're drunk and I don't want to take advantage of you in this state, you'll hate me in the morning," he has a sad look on his face.

So do I. I am drunk and the chances of me regretting this in the morning are slim to nil because all I want is him.

This withdrawal has been going on for too long. I can't take it anymore.

"Alright, I'm drunk, but I wasn't drunk at my birthday party. You never talked about that night. Why?"

His eyes widen. "Please, let's not talk about this here."

"Why not?" I look around us. There aren't many people around.

"Because we can't, come." He takes me by my arm and drags me with him out of the basement. I would have declined, but I had to rethink my choice: I don't want to talk about my not-so-existent love life in front of strangers because not all of them are drunk.

He leads us upstairs to the room where we first entered when we got here. When inside, he closes the door and starts pacing the room. "Funke look it's not like I don't like you or anything, I do and I think I'm falling in love with you, but the point is, you're still healing from everything and I know that being in a relationship with you is going to hurt you m–"

I cut in, "how is it going to hurt me?"

He sighs and tugs at his already messy hair, "when I kiss you or touch you, one way or the other, the memories are going to come flooding back and I can't be the one to do that to you, I can't let you go through the emotional torture because I'm too selfish to let you go."

He has a point, a very valid point, and I can't help but see it too. Defeated, I nod and sit on the bed. It's not that he doesn't reciprocate my feelings, he just doesn't want to hurt me by asking for a relationship. Why is my life like this? Why can't I just enjoy my newfound youth? I know I won't be able to handle the memories, so I won't try.

Adrian sits beside me. "Funke, I'm willing to wait for you till you get better, even if it means forever."

He hugs me and I hug him back like he is my life support. "Can we go home now?" I say into his shoulders.

He nods and separates himself from me. He takes my hand in his and leads us out of the room. Right now, all I need is sleep.

Back in the security of our small three-bedroom apartment, I am standing inside my bathroom, looking at myself in the mirror while Adrian fixes a late meal for us.

SAVING HER

My eyes are finally finding some color, and that brings a weak smile to my face. My hair, which has grown longer in the past weeks, now reaches my waist. I reach out to touch it. I am lucky with my hair. It is naturally soft despite having a lack of relaxer plus my mum's extra treatments for my hair and I don't have a problem growing the hair.

"Funke…" I don't hear the rest of his words because my knees weaken, causing me to grip the sink, and my stepfather's voice fills my ears.

Chapter Twelve

"Funke!" The man that I loathed with everything in me called and with a heavy sigh, I made my way downstairs. When I got to the living room, I found him sitting on the edge of the couch with his eyes fixed on the TV with the remote in his hand.

"Sir?" I gritted my teeth, hating to have to call him *sir*.

"Since when are you permitted to bring guests to the house?"

"Sir?" This time around, I called him *sir* because I was genuinely confused.

"Since when are you permitted to bring guests to the house?" He repeated and I knew I was hearing correctly.

Guests? I didn't invite anyone over. Adrian could never come over unannounced, so it couldn't be him. Who could it be?

"I didn't invite anyone over," I said truthfully.

"Then why is there a guy outside who claims that you have a project to work on together?" He suddenly stood up, his six-foot frame towering over me.

Project. It had to be Mide.

I didn't remember telling him to come over, but I remembered he was at the party. What the hell was he doing at my house? Fear washed over me and I shook my head. I knew I was six feet under already.

"I never told him to come, I swear."

"You swear?" He kept taking steps forward and I had to keep moving backward till my back was against the wall.

"I'm sorry." I swallowed the lump in my throat.

He raised his hand, causing me to close my eyes as I expected him to hit me, but what I felt were his fingers on my left cheek, slowly caressing it.

I flinched when I realized what he was doing. He gripped my chin and forced me to look up at him. "You're lucky I like you, so I'm going to let you off with a warning.

Never try this again." His palm came down on my cheek, hard; the sound echoed throughout the house and my cheek throbbed from the pain. I didn't make a sound until I was sure he was upstairs.

"Fuck," I gingerly touched my cheek, feeling the heat from the impact. "I'm going to kill this guy."

I stomped to the kitchen and went straight for the freezer. I took out a bag of ice and pressed it against my cheek so it wouldn't swell up instantly. After waiting for two minutes, I dumped the ice in the bag into the sink and went to open the door.

"What are you doing here?"

He turned around and smiled. "Hey you didn't get my text?"

I bit my bottom lip in frustration and looked away for a second. "I asked what you are doing here."

"For the project, remember we have to submit it." He answered, still with that irritating smile on his face.

"I know about the bloody project! What are you doing here? Did I ever agree with you to come here?" I was tempted to close the door and step out, but the fear of what my stepfather might say and do if he knew I did it was what stopped me.

"You don't remember? After your party that night, I texted you and you said to meet today. So I'm here," he shrugged as if he didn't just cause trouble for me.

"I was drunk that night and YOU TEXTED ME? YOU FUCKING TEXTED ME!" I yelled and he flinched. "Couldn't you use your common sense?" I touched the side of my head with my forefinger, poking at it twice. "To know that you should call or text again when I'm sober to confirm your plans?"

"I'm sorry, I didn't know." He shifted back. "I just thought–"

"Then you thought wrong." I shifted to the side to give him room to enter the house.

He still stood there and I rolled my eyes, "get in." I said, and he shyly walked into the house and I locked the door.

I led him to the dining room and told him to sit while I went to get my books. On my way up the stairs, I met my stepfather descending the stairs. I stepped to the side to let him pass.

He stopped by my side. "Try anything stupid and you'll pay for it." He whispered before walking away.

I waited until I heard the front door close before I continued up the stairs. I quickly picked up my schoolbag that was seated on my chair and the novel we were to work on that was on the table and ran back downstairs, thanking God when I met Mide as I had left him.

"Funke, I'm sorry for offending you." He said as I sat on the other side of the table away from him.

I wouldn't lie, it scared me to be alone in the house with him. I mean, I barely even knew him. What if he tried to rape or touch me? I already had enough of assaults in my life. I had thought my stepfather would still be in so I wouldn't have to be worried that he would try shit, at least because there would be someone in the house with us, but now that he had gone out, the fear worsened.

Should I call Adrian?

But what if I did and my stepfather arrived sooner than I imagined? What would I say then?

"Funke I'm so sorry, whatever you want I'll do." He apologized again and I looked at him, zoning out of my thoughts.

100

"Forget it." I waved my hand dismissively and turned my attention to my books.

After one long hour, we took a break since we were both tired. I ordered pizza and while we were waiting; I sat on the couch with my phone in hand. Mide finally stood up from his seat in the dining and walked toward me.

"Please, where's the restroom?"

I pointed towards the foyer where the guest bathroom was located, and he nodded, going there.

Two minutes after he was out and he sat beside me. I first looked at him before shifting to the other end of the couch to keep as much distance between us. I didn't want to look rude, which was why I didn't move to the armchair to my left.

He cleared his throat, "so, are you and Adrian like a thing?"

"No," I shook my head.

I felt his eyes on me and I shifted slightly.

"I always thought that you were mute and you only talked to Adrian." He chuckled and I rolled my eyes.

"Oh," I said, only to fill the awkward silence.

After a long minute of silence, the doorbell finally rang and I stood up at the same time he did.

"Here you go," I gave the delivery man the money after I pulled it out of the back pocket of my jean shorts. I closed the door and turned around, only to meet Mide standing there, the pizza box in my hand the only thing between us.

"What are you doing?" I looked at him warily.

"Nothing," he shrugged, as if he wasn't invading my personal space.

I walked away from him but still had my ears up and my body ready to defend myself. Even though I was defenseless against my stepfather but with this one, I wouldn't just stand back if he tried bullshit. Maybe I should have allowed Adrian to come over. I would have felt way more comfortable and I would sneak him out if my stepfather got back earlier than usual.

"I wanted to pay for that," Mide said, now behind me and I turned around so quickly, shocked to find him there.

"And I paid for it, so don't bother." I noticed he was now awfully closer to me.

I took a step back, but my back hit the edge of the dining table.

Shit.

"What are you doing?" I couldn't breathe and I wished I could just disappear.

He said nothing, but before I could process what was going on, he had my body pressed to his and he was kissing me. He gripped my chin to keep my face in place.

I pushed him with all the strength I could muster, but he was stronger than me, too strong that he didn't budge. His body felt like it was made of stone, so I resorted to my only other defense. I raised my leg and hit him square in the groin.

He pulled away instantly, crouching over. I wiped my mouth with the back of my hand, feeling disgusted. I packed his books into his bag and threw them at his still crouching figure.

"Get out of my house!" I yelled, pointing to the front door.

He slowly stood up after a while and he now looked at me. "You're beautiful." He said with a sick smile on his face.

"Fuck you!" My hand remained pointed at the door. "Now get out!"

"I can treat you better than Adrian ever will." he picked up his bag from the floor. "Think about it,"

I watched him walk out of the house and immediately the door closed behind him, I ran to it and locked it before sliding to the floor. This was why I hated guys. I told myself not to cry as I sat on the floor with my legs pulled up to my chest. I stood up for myself today and that counted for something.

When I could no longer feel my legs, I finally stood up and went upstairs to dip myself in the bathtub. I first brushed my teeth twice before stripping in front of the mirror in my bedroom and examining myself.

"You're beautiful."

His words replayed in my head.

Was I beautiful?

I looked at my naked form but saw no beauty there. All I saw was a beaten-up and weak body. I was very sure he said that because he wanted something, something he could never get.

SAVING HER

Done with my self-evaluation, I got into the bathroom and turned on the bathtub water to fill it up. I added my regular bath oils and made sure that the temperature was good enough for me before I got in.

Lagos

Chapter Thirteen

Inter-house sport was finally here, and I looked forward to the peace of mind I'd be getting after it. Before now, I'd have completely bailed on it, but I had a duty to my house that I had to fulfill. I had not just one but three races to run, so I couldn't afford to not be there. My house depended on me because I was the fastest girl, not in the house but in the school in its entirety.

Heat, a pre-inter house sports event, had happened two weeks ago, and I ran with the fastest students in senior school. During heat, every house brought two athletes and participants for an event and they all ran together. The house that comes fourth in the race doesn't get to run or take part in that event on the D-day. That day, I got the chance to run with guys too because they were curious about how fast I could run, that was the first time I had used all of my speed and I could match up to Adrian, the only reason I ever agreed to run with boys. Adrian was the fastest guy in the school and for me to match up with him, made all the other houses lose hope.

The first thing I did when I woke up was to go for my morning run. I used to run before, but I wasn't so committed to it. Now that I was involved in the sport, keeping fit was a necessity, so I had to stay committed. When I got back home, my stepfather was already sitting in the kitchen, his usual cup of tea in his hand. I had greeted him before I stepped out earlier, so there was no need to greet him again.

"Your mother told me you have this inter-house sports today." He was the first person to speak.

"Yes." I took out a bottle of water from the fridge and gulped it down.

"Are you competing in anything?"

His sudden interest in my school life shocked me. He had never asked about it.

"Yes, I'm running." I didn't look his way as I re-capped the bottle and stored it back in the fridge.

"Good. At least you're doing something with your life." He picked up his phone that was lying on the counter along with his cup of tea, then stood up and walked out of the kitchen. I breathed a sigh of relief as he walked out, and I hurried upstairs to get ready before he could come back downstairs and rape me.

After showering and changing into the sportswear, which was a white polo and white shorts that had the school logo and name inscribed on them, I wore my latest Nike trainers and packed my hair up in its regular ponytail. I packed an extra pair of clothes and trainers in my bag, along with a small towel. When I got downstairs, I threw in a few snacks from the pantry and two extra bottles of water, plus my regular water bottle that had more ice.

I was driving today, so I had brought my key down from my room today. Ever since I got the car, I never kept the key downstairs because of the fear of my stepfather driving the car. I walked right past him in the living room without saying a word to him and neither did he say anything to me too.

By the time I arrived at school, the field and bleachers were littered with people. I found my house's tent and the first person I recognized under the tent was Adrian. He stood up from his chair and met up with me.

"You made it." He hugged me and took my bag from my shoulders.

"What's that supposed to mean?" I frowned.

"I thought you'd bail on us today," he joked, and I playfully hit his arm.

The athletes huddled up in a corner, so I sat with them and listened to them as they talked. No, I didn't make any new friends, but compared to earlier times; they weren't looking at me like I was an abomination anymore. They all learned to ignore me rather than stare at me all day long.

"So," Mrs. Balogun was calling everyone's attention, and we all turned to look at her. "The first event is the march past after that long jump, then swimming and finally running, so let's all get ourselves prepared."

A few minutes after, the event officially started and everyone but the athletes and those competing in a sporting activity took their place in the bleachers. All houses, White, Blue, Red, and Green, had their tents pitched beside all four sides of both bleachers. The spaces reserved for each house had enough seats for the students to sit on the bleachers, and that way, the parents and other guests were between both houses on the bleachers.

The march past began, and we all watched, some cheering them on. Adrian, being a lot more social than me, joined them to cheer for our house when it was their turn. When the Long Jump had started, I was tired of sitting there, so I told Adrian that I was going to wait in my car and that he should call me when it was time to run.

"Where did you park?" He asked, holding my hand to stop me from moving further.

"Car Park B," I pointed to the said car park, and he nodded.

"I'm coming," he let go of me and I walked away.

As I got to my car, a familiar figure appeared beside me and I groaned. "What do you want now?"

"So you own a car?" She asked, shocked.

"Yes." I unlocked the car and got in. I started the engine and wound down all the glasses.

"Your car or your parents?" Once again, her voice was irritating me.

"My car. What do you want?" I turned, so I was facing her completely while still sitting in the driver's seat.

"Are you and Adrian a thing?" That question is the one question I had been getting since they pushed me to join inter-house sports practice.

"No."

"Good," she smiled.

I frowned, confused why she was smiling, and then it hit me. She wanted Adrian back, and she thought I would be a problem. Well, she was right. I would be a problem because I didn't want it to happen. Apart from the crush I had on him, he doesn't deserve someone like her.

I laughed. "Is that all?"

"No," she shook her head and stepped closer. "Just a fair warning; keep your claws off him. I don't care if he's your best friend because I get what I want and I want him, so back off."

I remained quiet. After waiting for an answer and getting nothing, she huffed and walked away.

"Bitch." I muttered and closed my car door, then turned off the engine. I tilted the chair backward so I could relax better.

Five minutes after, Adrian joined me in the car. "Hey," he tilted his seat just like I had done.

"Hey, what's happening now?" I pointed in the field's direction where the event was happening.

"Still at the long jump. What did Jasmine want?"

"She wants you," I said plainly. "Wait, how did you know?" I turned to him now.

He was looking at the small mirror in front of him as he adjusted his hair, pushing it back and forth. "I was on my way here and I saw her from afar, but then I remembered I had to do something, so I had to turn back." He was looking at his lips now and my mind went back to the night we kissed. He had said nothing about it since and I didn't know how I was going to bring up the topic.

He turned to me and licked his lips, "sad because I don't want her."

"How in your right senses did you fuck that girl?" I frowned. The thought of it angered me.

"Hey, she's hot alright? And I needed a fuck buddy, and she was there so," he shrugged and went back to looking at his face.

I wouldn't describe Jasmine as hot, but she sure was beautiful, and she had a decent body. It was just so sad that she slept around.

"Hey, I'm not in any way getting involved with her again." He assured me and my heart fluttered.

"I trust you, you have sense." I went back to my phone.

I was scrolling through Instagram because I had nothing better to do. I was already tired of waiting and I still had a few hours to go before my race. I should have stayed at home a bit longer.

"Let's go watch them swim," Adrian suggested, and I shook my head.

"Come on." He pouted. "Have you ever been there, to the pool?"

"Of course."

"Let's just go, please?" He pulled the baby-face on me and I looked away, refusing to give in. I just wanted to run my race and go home. I was tired already.

"Please, I'll buy you ice cream," he pressed his palms together.

I sighed, giving in. "I hate you,"

I adjusted my seat, so it was back to its original position. After winding up all the glasses of the car, I walked with Adrian into the school's main building.

As we sat on the bleachers and watched students dive in and out of the pool, people cheered them on, and it felt like my head was going to explode from the noise. Green House won the event like they always did. For the five years that I had been in secondary school, Green House always won the swimming event, so I was far from surprised.

Just as they were rounding up, Adrian and I left the pool and went to wait under our house's tent for the races to start. The housemistress and master huddled all athletes together and gave us the usual pep talk before pushing us all to join the other athletes at the starting line. They arranged us according to our schools: junior and senior schools. Junior girls started first, then junior boys before senior girls. The race was easier than I thought. I didn't have to put in so much effort and speed, and I still crossed the finish line before every other person. After the Red Cross made sure I was okay, I went back to wait for the 200 meters race. I crushed that one also, and I still had to sit back and wait for the relay race to start.

At the end of the day, I was exhausted, and all I wanted to do was go home and sleep. I had already said goodbye to Adrian, and I was getting to my car when I heard my name loud and clear. I turned around, confused. Why my name was called through the speakers?

"Funke, your cup," Adrian was now running towards me.

"My cup?" I furrowed my brows in confusion.

"Yes, for *female athlete of the year*." He stretched his hand forward, and I took it and let him drag me.

Adrian took my bag and car key from me and I was told to climb on the elevation that wrote '1'st.' They handed me the said cup, and the photographers took pictures and I was told to smile. I forced a small one and held the cup in front of me as they took pictures before I stepped down and took my bag and key from Adrian. I waited for him as he took his cup too for 'male athlete of the year.' They also made both of us take pictures together.

"My mum is here," he informed me as we began walking back to the car park.

"Where is she?" I adjusted my bag so I could hold the cup and my car key better.

"In her car, come on."

Once again, he held my hand and dragged me along with him.

I easily spotted his mum's car. Mrs. Parker was sitting in her car and her wandering eyes darted to Adrian and me as we got closer to her.

She got down from the car and pulled me in for a hug. "I heard, congratulations."

I didn't enjoy hugging people, but I didn't mind hugging her. I had started seeing her as a second mother. "Thank you ma,"

"How are you today?" She asked, holding my shoulders and her eyes studying my face.

"I'm okay," I nodded.

"Where's your mum or dad?" She looked around as if they would magically appear.

"They couldn't make it," I lied. The answer should have been: They don't have that kind of time for me.

I told my mum about the inter-house sports and she told her husband, so it was not a case of not being aware. Mum told me she was still in Abuja so she couldn't make it and my stepfather, we all know why: he's a piece of shit.

"Do you mind coming over? I cooked." She looked at Adrian as if asking for his help.

"Please?" Adrian smiled at me.

I chuckled, not able to resist both mother and son's charm. "Okay."

"Great, get in then," she got into her car and started the engine.

"I came in my car," I pointed to my car, which was not too far from where we were standing.

She looked at the car, then at me, and nodded. "Okay, I guess I'll see you at home."

I nodded. Adrian and I watched her drive off.

"I'll be behind you guys," Adrian said.

I walked toward my car and got in.

117

Lagos

Chapter Fourteen

"Funke! Get your ass here!" My stepfather yelled, making me jump from my bed. His voice always scared me.

I dragged my feet to his room and tried to think of a reason he called me, but came up short. When I got to his room, he was sitting on the bed, his door wide open.

"You called me?" I crossed my arms.

"Yes I did," he stood up, going around me and locking the door. He stood in front of me. "So, because you are now eighteen, you think you can do whatever you want?" He roughly gripped my face, "or because dear mummy threw you a party huh, answer me!" He yelled and roughly let go of my face.

"What is your point here?" I asked him, while trying to keep my hands from wiping my face.

"I'm just going to get straight to the point. I saw you kissing that boy. Why did you do that?"

My heart was supposed to be beating faster than normal, but somehow it wasn't. I was calmer than I should have been for some unknown reason. Maybe turning eighteen gave me a sense of courage to stand up for myself and a realization that if I wanted to stand up for myself, I actually could.

"Because I can. How has that got to do with you?" I was walking on eggshells here, but I would not back down, not now.

"Oh, it has everything to do with me. Do I need to spell it out for you? You belong to me, and no one else." His hand reached out to touch my face, but I moved away from him.

"I don't belong to you or anybody, I can d–" I didn't get to finish my brave speech because his hand met my face, painfully.

I cupped my cheeks and turned to him with an icy glare. If looks could kill, he would be six feet under by now.

"I don't need to repeat myself now, do I?" He reached out to touch my shirt, but I created a larger gap between us. "Now strip," he ordered.

I stood up straight, looking him in the eyes, "hell no." I refused.

Another slap landed on my cheek, and this time around, I didn't hold my face. I looked right back at him, feeling this unknown courage from wherever. I didn't know where this courage came from, but it made me feel good about myself. Even though he was still going to rape me in the end, I knew deep down that I stood up for myself more than I ever did in the past. That had to count as something.

He was quick to grab my shirt and before I knew it; it was in two, no longer on my body.

"No!" I screamed at him, trying to stop him, but that only seemed to encourage him as he laughed.

"Do I need to get the other one for you?" He asked, cocking his head to the side and looking like the maniac that he was.

SAVING HER

I didn't respond, but held onto my chest as my hands tried to cover my body. He took my silence as a go-ahead to get rid of my shorts and he reached for my zipper, undid everything, and pulled my shorts down. I tried everything I could, punch, kick, slap, bite, even spat on him, but like the maniac that he was, it only encouraged him.

"Now, do I need to do the rest of the work?"

I tried to calculate my escape. I could jump out through the balcony, rush to my car, and drive the hell out of this place. He couldn't jump out of the window after me and the gates were automatic so one push of a button and the gates would open, I always had spare clothes in my trunk since I got the car and the spare key hidden under an interlocking block close to where I parked the car.

It was my mother's birthday gift for me and I was more than happy when I saw the car. It was a beautiful all-black Venza, really great to drive.

Without thinking, I rushed to the balcony, but this man was faster than I thought. Before I could even phantom what was going on, he grabbed me and pulled me back.

121

"Where do you think you're going? Do you think you can run away? Think again." He turned me around so fast and ripped my bra off of my chest; the hook that held it to my chest snapped, and he forcefully pulled it off of my chest.

Damn it! I loved that bra.

He pushed me to the floor, making me land on my butt, hard. I covered my exposed chest with my hands and growled at him. Screaming will only make him continue. Maybe keeping quiet will make him release me.

"Take it off." He ordered.

I looked at my body, then at him and shook my head, "no." I spat.

"Why do you like making everything difficult?" He charged toward me.

I stood up from the floor as quickly as possible, still covering my chest with my hand. Even if he had seen me completely naked countless times, I still had my pride. I ran in circles around his room up to three times with him hot on my trail. The room was fairly big, so it was an exceptional exercise. I was trying to tire him out so that when he slowed down, I could run out of the room and it looked like it was working.

I suddenly slipped on something and I landed on the floor, face first, but one of my hands went ahead of the rest of my body and cushioned the fall. A sharp pain ran through my left hand as I rolled to the side. I had just broken my hand and it hurt like hell.

My stepfather roughly picked me from the ground and in the process dragged my left hand, causing a scream to leave my lips. I couldn't hold it in as the tears left my eyes. The pain was too much. I felt like I would pass out soon.

"Who do you think you are to play such stupid jokes with me?" He slapped me and I fell to the floor again.

I didn't have it in me to fight anymore. Whatever he wanted to do, he should do. I gave up.

He picked me up with my left hand again as a scream shook me. He slapped me again and this time I didn't feel the pain of my body hitting the ground because everything went black.

Chapter Fifteen

My fists head straight for my mirror in front of me and it shatters instantly. I don't stop. Punching it till every piece of glass is on the floor. I crouch and pick up a small piece, turning the sharpest side to my wrist.

I can't do this anymore. I can't have a normal life because some bastard raped me for years, and I can't even date the person I like because there is a high tendency I could break even more than I already have. Maybe ending my life will end the torture.

My hands are shaking as I bring the glass to my wrist and apply pressure. My brain registers the pain, but it is the farthest thing from my mind. All I can think of is leaving this world.

I am ready for this.

SAVING HER

Blood pours from the wound and just as I am about to apply extra pressure and extend the glass, the door swings open and the glass is out of my reach. I am hoisted off the floor and pushed out of the room with Adrian's arms wrapped around me. He forces me to sit on the bed and quickly takes off his shirt and wraps it around my wrist, trying to stop the flow of blood. Like so many other things, I can't control my tears as they pour, the pain is too much. I lift my legs to my chest and curl up into a ball. I desperately want to disappear from the face of the earth.

Why did Adrian stop me?

Adrian wraps his arms around me again, assuring me of his presence as I rest my head on his chest. He weaves his hand through my hair as he speaks to me, telling me it will all be over soon. I wish I can believe him.

A few moments after, he takes my injured wrist and inspects it to be sure that the blood has stopped gushing out. He applies a little pressure and after like a minute; he stops to inspect the hand again. When satisfied, he draws me closer to him and plants a soft kiss on my forehead.

The tears don't stop, but the shaking does. I cry for as long as my eyes can produce the tears, then it all stops, leaving me numb. Adrian helps me to lie on the bed before laying down beside me and holding me close once again. My eyes feel heavy and I let the sleep take over.

The first thing my brain registers the moment my eyes shoot open is the smell of pancakes. I turn around on the bed and gasp when I see the bandage wrapped around my wrist. As if on cue, I feel the pain travels down my arm. I wince and sit up.

What the hell happened?

The memories of what happened flood my mind like a broken dam and I fight the tears that pool in my eyes. I blink them away, stand up from the bed, and walk to the bathroom before shutting the door behind me. The mirror on the wall is gone, and the floor is clean of any broken glasses.

Quickly brushing my teeth, I splash water on my face and run my hand through my messy hair. I do not know what I look like, but I know that it's not something anyone will want to see. I feel like shit and I am sure I look like shit.

Done in the bathroom, I step into the room and slip on my pair of blue fluffy slippers, then head downstairs, following the smell of pancakes and freshly ground coffee to the kitchen. Adrian hardly cooks, but once in a while, he cooks for me.

"Hey," I say when my eyes land on him from the door of the kitchen.

He turns around and a small smile stretches on his lips, "hi."

I take my seat on a stool by the island. Adrian slides over a plate of pancakes and the maple syrup over to me, then he makes my coffee and comes over to my side to give it to me.

"Eat up, you need it." He instructs and goes back to the stove.

Seconds after, he puts out the flames of the gas cooker and pushes his breakfast close to me, then sits down

127

beside me. I take the syrup and pour a generous amount over my pancakes before sliding the jug over to him.

"Did you sleep well?" He asks as he copies my action, but doesn't use as much syrup as me.

I nod, "I guess."

I stuff my mouth with the goodness in front of me and moan in delight when the taste of the food melts on my tongue. Adrian chuckles beside me and I glance at him before going back to my food. We eat in comfortable silence and when I'm done with my pancakes, Adrian speaks up.

"Your mum called."

I lift a brow. "Okay?"

"And she called your therapist. She should be here any minute," he finishes, and my face squeezes in discomfort.

I hate hearing about the therapist. She is my second worst nightmare. Having to sit down with someone for an hour and talk about how you feel. I am not very cooperative with her, but I have to deal with her either way; my mum pays heavily for her services. Frequently, it is an entire hour of me staring at the wall behind her, or the artworks hung on the walls of her office as she asks me questions that I never answer. Sometimes I would talk and tell her how I felt and that would be the end of the conversation for the day.

I reply to Adrian with a shrug and sip my coffee. He stands up and takes our plates to the sink to wash. When he is done, he sits down back, sipping his coffee too.

"About last night," he says, but I raise my hand to stop him from saying further.

"Please, the thera–"

This time, he stops me. "No, that's not what I want to talk about. Just listen." He sucks in a deep breath, "please never think of leaving me again, I beg you. I can't imagine my life without you." He drops his cup and mine on the counter after retrieving them from my hand. He takes my hand in his, the warmth soothing me, "please don't leave me, we're in this together, it's me and you, and I wouldn't imagine how it would be if you left."

The tears in my eyes finally fall, and he reaches out to wipe them for me. Adrian is worth sticking in this living hell for, even if that is the only thing I can give to him, I will stay alive for him. No guarantees, but I will try.

129

I drape my arms around his neck and pull him in for a hug. He hugs me back instantly. I nod yes at his request as I bury my head into his neck. A knock on the front door causes us to scramble from each other. Adrian stands up and goes to answer the door, so I quickly finish the rest of my coffee and wash the cup.

"Dr. Grey is here," Adrian announces as he walks back into the kitchen and picks up his cup of coffee, taking a large gulp from it.

I nod and give him a half-smile before heading to the living room where my therapist is. It is a Saturday and I'm not supposed to have a session with her but because of my episode yesterday, my mother had to be my mother. I'm sure Dr. Grey is getting an extra pay for this.

Today she wears a blue fitted skirt, a white off-shouldered shirt, and her signature black stilettoes. Sometimes I try to wonder how she walks in those shoes all day.

"Funke." She beams as I walk into the room.

"Hi Dr. Grey." I force a smile and take my seat opposite her.

"Enough with the formalities. I've told you to call me Arianna or Ana." her smile is soft, not fake.

I shrug, waiting for her to speak.

She clears her throat. "So, how have you been?"

I give her a blank stare. "Why don't you just get straight to the point?" I am tired of her pointless questions. She was called to my house for a reason, so she might as well get to it.

She sighs, "Alright, how do you feel about it? Do you regret it or do you wish Adrian didn't come in at the time he did?"

I feel bad about it and I regret it, only because I now realize that Adrian would have been alone if I left. I'm grateful that he came in at the time he did.

My lips remain sealed as I stare at her, waiting for the time to pass or for her to read my thoughts and get on with the next question. I never liked to answer her questions, and I probably never will.

"Okay, Adrian was really worried, your mum was worried, I was worried," she gives me a sad smile. "You're probably not going to talk to me during this session, but know that we all care about you."

131

"Why?" I breathe out, shocking both her and myself.

"Why do we care about you?" She asks.

I shake my head, "no."

"Why we were worried?" She asks and I look away from her, the window behind her suddenly becoming more interesting. "Well, we were worried because we all love you." She answers simply.

"I like him, you know, but we can't date." Why I am suddenly speaking to her today, I don't know, but I can feel the weight leaving my chest with every word I speak. Before, it felt like my chest was going to explode from how much I had kept in.

"Oh, you like someone," her eyes light up. "That's great."

"I'm probably never going to get married and have kids," I shake my head.

"Who says you can't? You can do whatever you set your mind to do. It may just take more time than you expect, but you can do it. I believe in you," she says, but I am done talking. "What happened to you in the past shouldn't be a determining factor of how the rest of your life must be." She adds.

When I don't respond, she continues to talk, but I don't listen. I zone out and imagine my life if everything didn't go downhill. I probably would be in the university, and Adrian would be my boyfriend, I would have sleepovers, go shopping with my girlfriends and talk about hot guys even if I was in a relationship.

The hour passes by quickly and soon enough she is out the door and I am still stuck in my seat.

Chicago

Chapter Sixteen

"Adrian!" I call out as I slip my phone into the pocket of my shorts. We are about to leave for work but Adrian is running a bit late today, something he never does. "Adrian!" I call out again.

I'm met with radio silence again, so I angrily stomp to his room. I lightly knock on his door before pushing it open. To my greatest surprise, Adrian is on his bed, dressed in black jeans and a white shirt. He is lying face down and he groans when he notices my presence in the room.

"Adrian, what's going on?" I rush to his side, trying to push him to look at me, worried that he might be ill.

He groans again before rolling over. "I don't want to go to work."

His hair is wet, his pillow confirms it, and his room smells of his perfume like he had just used it. "But you're dressed for work." I deadpan.

"That doesn't mean that I'm excited about it," he sits up.

I am confused, "why are you suddenly doing this?"

"I wish things were different." He stands up from the bed, and it's as if the old Adrian suddenly pops back. He puts on his Vans and puts his phone, which was on the table inside the front pocket of his jeans.

I stand up and move closer to him. "What is going on, Adrian?"

"Can I kiss you one last time?" He looks serious.

My mouth falls open in shock as I look at him quizzically.

"Please," he pleads, and closes the gap between us, pressing his body to mine. He cups my face in his hands and he leans in slowly. I don't push him away and neither do I do anything.

His lips capture mine, and I close my eyes to kiss him back. This kiss is different. It is slow and passionate, and it is like I can hear his every thought as our lips move in sync.

This is a promise to me: he will wait for me, even if it takes forever. I place my hands on his waist as he pulls me closer to him, if it is even possible. If it was possible to be inside his skin, I'm sure I'd be in now. I can feel his abs against my chest. My hands move to his neck while his hands drop to my hips. My head is swimming in euphoria and I want this more than anything, but I can't have it, not yet. I have a broken heart and mind to heal first.

We pull away from each other and we're both out of breath. I look into his eyes, enjoying the warmth and feeling of home it gives me. He gives me a quick kiss on my forehead before hugging me. I drop my head on his chest and close my eyes, relishing the moment.

"The movie we couldn't see the other day, let's go see it today." Adrian says to me as I fling my cross-body bag over my head so it is sitting across my chest.

"Sure." I nod and walk out of the store, Adrian behind me. "But why can't you go with one of your friends instead?" I ask, out of curiosity.

"They are all busy, planning another party," he rolls his eyes as he unlocks his car and we both get in.

Mainly because we were running late by the time we left the house, Adrian had to drive us to work. I didn't mind, though.

"Since today is Monday, the time for the movie is different, so instead of four, the movie starts at two, so we should head there first if we want to watch it at all," Adrian announces, and I nod. I have nothing else to do.

I push the radio button and *Unconditionally by Katy Perry* is playing. We sit in silence as the music floods the car. I unconsciously hum to the song as Adrian has his gaze fixed on the road. The cinema is far from our side of town, so it takes a while before Adrian puts the car to a final halt. I quickly unbuckle my seat belt and get out of the car. We walk into the building and join the line to get our tickets, popcorn, and drink.

The time on my watch is one forty-five pm. I shrug and look back up. I notice a couple beside us. They are holding hands and the guy is leaning into the girl and whispering something to her. The way she laughs when he's done talking has me admiring them. They are black and the guy has his hair in an 'afro mess' like I call it and his eyes are grey, not usual for a black person. Well, my eyes aren't the usual. The girl looks my way and studies me for a second before giving me a small smile and a wave to which I return. She looks friendly but I'm not one to start conversations, so I don't try.

"Soda?" Adrian asks, making me look at him. I didn't even notice that it was our turn on the line.

SAVING HER

"Coke," I answer, discarding manners when I go back to staring at the couple.

They are now at the front of their line, making their orders.

"Riya, what soda do you want?" The guy asks her.

Riya, that's a nice name, but she doesn't look Indian or Hindi or from that side at all. It is probably the short form of a name. Only Victoria and Gloria come to my head, so it has to be one of those two or none. I will never know anyway, so there is no need to sweat over it.

Adrian hands me the popcorn and my drink and we leave the line, going to sit in the waiting area. Shortly after, the cute couple comes over too and sits down at the table beside us. Having a closer look now, I notice how beautiful the girl is. Her hair is not as long and full as mine, but still full and long either way. It's packed up just like mine, highlighting her slim facial features. She's a true beauty and deep down, I get jealous. If only I can be happy and date the person I have feelings for like her.

"Funke, are you even listening to me?" Adrian snaps his fingers in my face, snapping me out of my silly daydream.

139

"Sorry, what did you say?" I finally tear my gaze from the couple.

He sighs and shakes his head before speaking. "I was telling you about the film, not that you care to know, anyway." The pain in his voice causes my heart to clench in guilt.

I gasp. "Don't say that. I care to know. It's just that, this is a movie you want to watch and whether I'm going to like the movie or not, I want to watch it with you so I don't care for the movie right now, I can figure out the name when we watch it or after. That's what best friends do for each other, right?" I hold his arm.

His gaze softens, "alright." He smiles a little.

Adrian talks to me about the film and what to expect from it. It sounds interesting and I am excited to watch it.

I don't look at the couple beside us or even notice them until they stand up at the same time that we do to go watch our movie. We are going to the same theater and when we get inside and sit down, only two seats are in between us.

Adrian doesn't seem to notice them, or he just refuses to say anything about it. I don't mind though; I mean, I may never see them again and my social skills are the worst at the moment.

Chicago

Chapter Seventeen

"Hi," the lady who was with her boyfriend from earlier says to me as Adrian and I walk out of the cinema; e just finished watching our movie. Her voice is firm, giving me the vibes that she is confident in herself, unlike me.

"Hi," I smile at her to cover the cringe my face was about to form. Just two letters and I nearly made a fool out of myself; my voice came out weak, unlike hers.

"I just wanted to say that I love your hair. What products do you use?" Her eyes hold warmth in them and I take in a breath to relax.

"Thank you," I smile inwardly when my voice comes out stronger than earlier. "I use Cantu leave-in conditioner and coconut oil," I answer and her eyes widen. I use more products than that but I can't start rambling about all of that. Those two I mentioned are the essentials.

"Coconut oil, I've heard how good it works," she nods with a grin. "Well, thank you." She walks away, going to meet her boyfriend.

I once again admire how cute they look together as I watch their retreating figures. I am hopeless.

"What are you looking at?" Adrian asks, reappearing beside me. He walked ahead of me when the lady started talking to me.

"Nothing." I shake my head and head to the car with Adrian.

"So, how was the movie?" He puts the car in reverse and looks at the rearview mirror before stepping on the gas.

I wait till we've joined the main road before speaking. "It was nice, I liked it actually," I answer honestly, and that brings a smile to his face.

"I'm glad you did." he pushes the radio button and changes the channel when we hear two people having a conversation.

The song that comes on is unfamiliar to me, but I like how it sounds. "We should go out again soon," I say.

"Sure, anytime you want to."

Our neighborhood soon comes into view and my legs itch to get into the house and throw myself on the bed. I missed it. When the car comes to a final halt, I'm the first to get out of the car and into the house. The house is silent as expected, but I feel something is off.

"Oh, you guys are back!" My mother says, startling me.

I reach for the light switch and flick it on. She is standing at the top of the stairs looking as casual as ever in yellow shorts and a grey tank top.

"Woman, you scared me." I take off my shoes. "What are you doing here?" I head to the kitchen at the same time Adrian walks into the house and freezes upon seeing my mother.

"Aunt Dianne," he quickly takes off his shoes. "This is a surprise."

"Yeah," I roll my eyes and turn on the kitchen tap to wash my hands first before drying them and turning to look at my mother.

SAVING HER

There goes my plan of marrying my bed tonight. I don't exactly like my mother despite how I acted when we were around people, but Adrian wasn't just people, plus I can't hide this from her. The reason it shocked me when she threw me that birthday party was because she never had time for me, always busy with one stupid business or the other, but I don't complain since that brings food to the table.

I don't like her mainly because of her negligence of me, if she is the regular mum, even with her busy schedule, the mother who calls as often as she can, the mother who surprises you with her presence and takes you shopping regularly, the one who braids your hair while you talk about boys, the mother who you would have a mani-pedi appointment in the salon with, none of the bullshit in my life would have happened.

I won't have PTSD to deal with. I would be in the university, attending boring lectures. Adrian and I would be a couple and I wouldn't be socially awkward.

She caused the mess I call my life, so yes, I have every right to not like her. Shortly before we came to Chicago, we had a heart-to-heart talk, and I thought she would change, but I was wrong. She went back to being the mother I've known from age eight.

"Funke, the least you could do is pretend to be excited to see me," my mother raises her voice a little.

"Oh, I did. That's why you're still inside the house." I rest my weight on the counter, my palms spread out on it.

"Funke," Adrian warns, giving me a look that said I should stop talking.

"A house that I bought for you," my mother points out.

I ignore Adrian. "You wouldn't have had to do so if you—"

Adrian clamps his hand on my mouth, stopping me from speaking further. "Alright that's enough, let's get you upstairs." His hand remains over my mouth as he walks upstairs with me.

I don't spare my mother another glance as we walk past her, but I know she is fuming. She should have expected that when she showed up unannounced. When we get to the room, Adrian finally lets go of my mouth and glares at me.

"Look, I know you're pissed, but she's still your mother and you should respect that," he tells me and I sit on the bed.

"Whatever." I roll my eyes and dramatically fold my arms across my chest.

He sits down beside me, "Funke please just try, for me. She'll leave soon and then we can be alone again, please?"

I turn my body to look at him and drop my hands to my lap. "Alright, but only because you asked nicely."

He smiles, "thanks."

"I'm hungry," I change the topic.

"I was thinking of pizza. What do you think?"

I scoff, "with that woman down there, you think you can eat pizza as dinner? I wouldn't be surprised if she came along with a meal that might be in the fridge."

"Alright, what do you suggest we eat?" He crosses his arms over his chest.

"I have no idea Adrian, all I know is that I'm hungry so provide food." I stand up from the bed and walk to my closet.

"See this one," his Nigerian accent seeps in. "Do you think I'm your chef or what?" Adrian is suddenly behind me.

I turn to look at him with my black Nike shorts in my hands. "Yes," I smirk.

"Oh, really?" He smirks too, coming closer to me.

I notice how close we are. If he moves just a little closer, our lips will be touching. I look up at his eyes and they hold something that I have become all too familiar with: lust. This is becoming a regular thing and we tell ourselves that a relationship isn't good for us.

"Yes," I whisper, and he closes the gap between us, smashing his lips on mine.

I kiss him back for only a second before pulling away and resting my hands on his chest. "My mum is downstairs." I say.

He rolls his eyes, "and so? She's not coming in here," he reminds me.

I sigh. "Adrian, we can't continue like this. It isn't what we agreed on."

"Fine." he stretches the space between us, his mood completely changed. "I'll go ask your mum what she wants to have for dinner." He leaves the room.

I quickly change into the shorts in my hand, and a yellow tank top, and I head downstairs.

Lagos

Chapter Eighteen

I woke up with a start and my head collided with something before my back met the cold bed. No, it couldn't have been the bed, it was too hard. I turned to my side, and I noticed I was on the floor, not only on the floor, the floor under my stepfather's bed. I was grateful it was clean today.

I reached out to touch my burning forehead, but the pain I felt in my hand stopped me, making me scream. My left hand felt out of place, and dare I say, broken. With the way I hit my head, I was sure it was swelling.

I crawled my way out from under the bed and let me tell you; it was not funny. With a broken hand and a swollen forehead, it felt like I was going to pass out again.

After I passed out, he woke me up and raped me, then pushed me to sleep under his bed.

Evil much.

The night sky was already on the surface and from where I sat on the floor, I could see the stars. I got up from the floor and walked out of the room. The house was silent, which was strange. I first went into my room to put on some clothes before heading downstairs, but I didn't find anyone, not even my stepfather. The housekeeper had gone home by then, so it was supposed to be only me and him.

I checked every other place in the house that I thought he could be, but he wasn't there, so that left me with no option but to look for his car. I went outside, and it did not surprise me when I didn't find his car. He was probably out drinking.

I went back upstairs and found my phone ringing, but before I could pick it up, it went off. I unlocked the phone, and I saw twenty missed calls and fifteen messages from Adrian. His messages were a bunch of *'where are you?'* *'Are you okay?'* *'Hope everything is fine.'* I had completely forgotten that we were chatting before the devil incarnate called me to his room earlier. I didn't want to call Adrian back just yet because I didn't have the strength to explain, so I just plugged in my phone. An idea popped into my head and I paused what I was doing for a second.

Maybe I should use this opportunity to run away. I would go to Adrian's house and my stepfather would never know where I went. That could work. I had my driver's license and with my broken arm, which hurt like hell, that would be a good excuse for any police officer I could meet on the road. Adrian's mother was a nurse, so she could help me when I get there.

Since I had an emergency kit in my car with everything I would need for two weeks in it, I didn't need to take anything from the house. All I needed was my charger, phone, headphones, and car keys and I was good to go. I took my favorite hoodie from my wardrobe with my needed items and ran out of the room.

I had better leave before he came back. I didn't know how long he had been away. When I got to the living room, I took my car keys and the remote to the gate along with me and ran out of the house.

I quickly unlocked my car and got in, starting the engine. Even though I had just one good hand, I was still going to drive myself out of that place. When I drove to the gate, I opened it and honked for the gateman to come out so I could give him instructions.

He ran out of his house, running to the passenger's door. I wound down the passenger's glass, *"I wan go buy Suya. If oga come back and e no ask for me, no tell am anything oo!"* I warned and with my one good hand, I reached into my purse and took out two thousand Naira and gave it to him.

"Ah no wahala madam, thank you oo. Drive safely o." He took the money from me while slightly bowing his head in appreciation.

I didn't reply again as I wound up the glass and drove out of the compound. This was it. I was finally free. I drove as fast as I could, not going over the speed limit.

I didn't know what was going to happen when I got to Adrian's house, but one thing was sure: I was not going back to that house until justice was served. I was going to tell Adrian the truth, and he was going to help me, him, and his mum.

I got to a traffic light, and I had to stop because I was making a U-turn. I looked ahead of me and just after the streetlight at the opposite U-turn point, I saw a car that I could recognize anywhere: my stepfather's car. I froze and said a prayer that he wouldn't spot my car or recognize it from his mirrors.

The sound of a car horn startled me. The traffic light was green when I stepped on the gas. I believed my stepfather was heading home, and he was going through the second route that led to the house. I had never been happier that I left the house the moment I did.

I honked when I got to the gate to Adrian's house and seconds after, the gateman came outside to look at who was there. I dimmed my lights so he could see it was my car and when the realization hit, he nodded and smiled. He opened the gate.

When I drove in, I parked my car behind Adrian's and got out of the car with my purse that had my charger and headphones, then put my phone in my pocket. I took out my bag from the trunk of the car and locked the car.

"Funke?" I heard Adrian call out just before I turned around to look at him.

"Hey. I would say I'm sorry for disturbing you this late, but I'm not because I need your help," I said as I walked toward him.

His eyes scanned me from head to toe and his jaw, not for once, left the floor. I rolled my eyes at him and grabbed his arm as I walked towards his front door, him behind me. "If you're shocked by what you're seeing now, then you won't believe what I'm going to tell you."

I didn't bother taking off my shoes as I walked into his house and straight to his kitchen. I dropped my bag on the counter and opened his fridge to get a bottle of water, doing all that with my right hand.

Adrian noticed this and asked me what was wrong. I lifted my forefinger before gulping down the water. I wiped my chin with the back of my hand when I was done and dropped the almost empty bottle on the counter.

"Funke?" His mother spoke, appearing from the living room, "I know I hear–" she paused and I looked at her, "why is your left hand at an awkward angle?" She asked while walking closer to me, "and why is your forehead swollen?"

She reached out to hold my broken arm, causing me to yell in pain. "Is it broken?" She asked me.

"It feels like it," I answered, looking at Adrian to gauge his reaction.

"What the fuck happened to you?" Adrian asked, his nose flaring in anger.

"Language, boy." She nodded at me. "Come with me."

She walked out of the kitchen first, but before I could take one step, Adrian was quick to stand in front of me. "Is this your stepfather?"

I nodded slowly. "Just let your mother patch me up and I'll tell you the full story." I gave him a fake smile as I bypassed him and walked to the living room.

Chapter Nineteen

"Let's play truth or dare," Dakota suggests.

We are all hanging out at Adrian and I's place. Dakota, Aiden, Derek, Josh, Lucy, Helen, Misses McClain's daughter, Adrian, and I are all seated in the living room, 'hanging out.' Helen got back from her trip to LA last week and she continued her work in the shop, so we got a little closer. Adrian's friends came over to the shop some time ago, so we all automatically formed a small group. They were to return to college in about a week, so everyone was trying to enjoy the last of their summer holiday.

No one objected to Dakota's idea of a game, so he is the first person to speak. "Helen truth or dare?"

"Dare," Helen answers almost instantly.

"I dare you to make out with Aiden," Dakota smirks.

Helen has a crush on Aiden, and she isn't hiding that fact. Aiden doesn't seem to mind Dakota's dare, because I think he has a crush on her, too.

Helen stands up from where she was sitting on the floor beside Lucy and walks to where Aiden is sitting. Aiden stands up too, his frame towering over her. He is a good 6'1 while Helen is somewhere between 5'5 and 5'7. I take my eyes away from them when they both lean in.

A whole minute after Dakota clears his throat and Helen goes back to her position. "Truth or dare Adrian?" Helen asks.

"Truth," Adrian replies.

"How do you feel about Funke?" Helen asks, making me look up at her first, then at Adrian.

He fixes his gaze on me as he speaks. "I like her a lot."

I'm not surprised, but everyone else in the room surely is. His bluntness surprises them. I'm sure they weren't expecting him to answer that way. I feel their gazes on me and then on Adrian. They are murmuring amongst themselves while Adrian and I maintain eye contact.

"Then why aren't you guys dating?" Aiden asks.

"It's complicated," I answer this time around.

"Lucy truth or dare?" Adrian quickly asks to change the subject.

I know that I'm having fun, even though I can't call all of them my friends, but it is still fun playing a game I had never played before with people that I don't know so much about.

My mum walks into the house, causing our laughter to seize.

"Oh, I'm so sorry, carry on," she walks upstairs with her bag in her hand, and seconds after, it's like she wasn't there at all. She has been staying with us this past week and let's just say it isn't my greatest joy, but I have to deal with it. She should be out of here by the end of the week. Work is always calling her.

"Whose mum is that?" Josh asks, and I chuckle.

"My mum," I say.

"You guys don't look alike," Derek points out.

"Oh I know," I nod.

Everyone who has met my mum and I know we don't look alike, maybe a few features here and there, but nothing so specific. Now if I don't look so much like her, then I surely look like my father, who we have no clue who he is.

Yay to me!

Adrian looks at the time on his watch, then at me, and I immediately know what that means. I have to go see my therapist. I roll my eyes and stand up, going to the kitchen.

"Uh guys, I think this is where we have to end it for today. Funke and I have duties to attend to at the moment," Adrian says, making them groan.

They all complain but stand up, filing out of the house one by one. Adrian and I say goodbye to them and when the last person is out of the house, I release a sigh of relief.

"Alright, we've got to get going." Adrian takes his car key from the coffee table. "Aunt Dianne, we're going out!" he yells so my mum can hear him.

She yells, "okay don't be home late." And that is our cue to leave. I reluctantly follow him out of the house. Going to the therapist is *not* the highlight of my day.

SAVING HER

An hour and a half later, we are back at the house. The appointment was the usual. She talks and I stare blankly at the wall, waiting for time to fly so I could get out of that place.

"Welcome, dinner is ready," my mum says when we walk into the house. She is sitting on the couch, the TV remote in her hands and her eyes glued to the TV.

"Alright, I'll be down in a few. I just need to take a shower," Adrian says before heading upstairs.

I am hungry and don't have it in me to take a shower first, so I drop my phone on the kitchen counter and wash my hands, ready to eat. I take a plate from the rack and open the pot. *Jollof* rice is staring back at me. To be honest, I've missed this meal.

I serve myself and turn to the bowl of fried chicken on the counter. I add one piece to my plate.

"Should I serve your food, mother?"

"Sure," from the corner of my eye I see her stand up and walk to the kitchen.

I quickly serve her food and set it on the counter. When I'm done, she's standing on the other side of the counter, looking at me.

"What?" I raise a quizzical brow at her and sit down on a stool.

"How are you? How was your day?" She asks, shocking the hell out of me. I nearly choke on my food.

"I'm fine and my day was fine," I answer and get up to take two bottles of water from the fridge before going back to my food.

"I see you're socializing better with people, that's great," she too sits down, waiting for my reply.

I slide a bottle of water to her. "Yeah, thanks to Dr. Grey," I say sarcastically, still avoiding her gaze.

"She's doing her job."

I want to laugh, but I hold it in. She doesn't understand at all. I don't care, anyway.

162

SAVING HER

Adrian reappears, and that is the end of the conversation.

Chapter Twenty

When I got to the living room, I sat down first and then took out my phone from my pocket. I gave the phone to Adrian, who sat beside me. "Help me break my SIM cards. I don't want him to find me." I told him.

He nodded and did as I asked him. His mum cleared her throat, successfully getting my attention. She took my left arm and shook it a little. I winced at the pain, so she stopped.

"Where does it hurt?" She asked.

"My elbow," I answered. She held my elbow, and I screamed in pain again.

She sat back before reaching to get the stool from the corner to sit in front of me. "This is going to hurt," she told me and, without warning, shifted my elbow back to the right position.

"FUCK!" I yelled as the pain shook through my body.

Adrian's mum eyed me first before she started patching up my arm. Adrian squeezed my thigh reassuringly, and I gave him a painful smile. When his mum was done with the cast, she gave me a sling to help me with it, too. Then she massaged my forehead with a balm before standing up to wash her hand, then came to sit down on my other side.

"I don't need to ask you to explain, do I?" She said, looking at me with a serious face.

Adrian had a serious face as well. I was ready to tell someone now. I took in a deep breath and for the first time since I knew Adrian, I told him everything and I mean everything.

When I was done, Adrian's mum stood up from where she sat and walked over to the bar in the room. She took out her phone from her pocket and started making calls.

"So you've been going through all these for long and you never told me?" Adrian asked, pain in his voice.

The guilt was eating at me, and I couldn't look at his face. "I'm sorry. I was just scared." My voice broke, making me sound like a broken record.

He carefully pulled me to his chest, making sure not to cause more pain to my broken hand. I rested my face on his chest, letting the tears fall and soak his shirt. His body shook with rage as he held me to his chest, "I'm always here for you, Funke, I am. Please promise me you won't keep such from me again. We're best friends and I love you."

I replied with a nod of my head as he still held me to his chest. His mother walked back to us and we pulled away.

"You are never going back to that house until he is behind bars. Give me your mother's number. I'm going to talk some sense into her this night." She said with a commanding voice, and I obeyed.

I gave her mother's number, at least the number I knew she would be reachable with now, and with that she went upstairs. Seconds after, her voice echoed throughout the house, "Adrian, give her food and whatever she wants, get the guest room ready because this is going to be her new home."

As ordered, Adrian took me to the kitchen, gave me food, no, he fed me. Took me to the guest room and asked if I needed anything before he left me to get ready for bed.

His mum gave me a waterproof cover for my cast so that I could shower without fear of getting it soaked. When I was done with the shower, I changed into a shirt and sweatpants and I was ready for bed. A few minutes after, Adrian's mother came in and gave me some painkillers and promised a proper check-up by the morrow. She promised a trip to the police station together with an organization that fights against gender violence and mostly rape.

By the time she finished talking, I was tired, so I laid on the bed and slept off almost instantly.

Chapter Twenty One

For the first time in ten years, I walked into the school building with my head up. I walked like everything in my life made sense, even though it didn't at the moment. Adrian walked by my side as we took the stairs one at a time.

We passed a few of my classmates on the way and it surprised some to see my full face or the cast pulled to my chest. I always used my hair to cover my face, or I just kept it low anytime I walked the school corridors, so what most people got was the lower part of my face.

I'm sure my heterochromia surprised them. In the past, the news was going around about it, but I never really cared. They got tired of asking me to show them and me declining or completely ignoring them, so they stopped altogether. I'm sure seeing my eyes now, people would pick up the topic again.

We walked into the class, and we sat down in our respective seats. I hung my bag pack over the chair and I took out my phone, something I never really used in school. As mentioned earlier, my school wasn't the average Nigerian school, so using my phone in school wasn't a crime.

I had a new message from Adrian's mum telling me they had taken my stepfather into custody for questioning and we would have to excuse ourselves from school during our lunch break to be questioned by the police, too. I told Adrian, and he nodded.

My nerves were all over the place, but I was happy at the same time. The justice I had been waiting for my whole life was being offered to me. My stepfather was going to rot in jail for his crimes.

The bell for assembly rang, and as usual, everyone filed out of their classrooms and straight to the school hall for the assembly. Adrian and I did the same as everyone else, walking together to the hall.

We joined our class line and shortly after, a student from my class went up to the podium and she started singing, so everyone who knew the song joined her. I didn't know the song, so I didn't sing.

The principal suddenly came up to the podium. "Good morning students. Funke Ayodeji and Adrian Parker, please report to my office."

I looked at Adrian, and he was looking back at me. I turned around and headed to the principal's office. When out of sight, Adrian took my hand in his, assuring me that everything was going to be fine.

We both didn't know why the principal suddenly summoned us to her office, but I wasn't scared because I had a clean record in the school. When we got to the front of the office, Adrian unlocked our hands and sent a nod to the receptionist before knocking on the door.

We both heard a 'come in' and Adrian opened the door, going in first. The office was the typical principal's office. Shelves filled with books and trophies, a cabinet, a desk with a few files on it, a few picture frames, and a scowling principal sitting behind the desk, her glasses resting on her nose.

"Good morning ma," Adrian and I greeted her.

"Good morning," she took off her eyeglass and pointed the tip at Adrian. "I just got a call from your mother requesting both your presence at her hospital for a medical checkup."

She gave Adrian a slip, "that's your gate pass." She waved us off.

Adrian and I left the office without saying another word to her.

Adrian was the first to speak. "That was quick."

We took the stairs two at a time.

"Good, I'm tired of this place already," I said in relief. I was getting irritated by the stares and murmurs all around. Even teachers couldn't hold themselves.

Adrian chuckled and shook his head as we walked back into our class. As fast as possible, we took our bags from our seats and left the school building and went into Adrian's car. Since I spent the night at his house, he drove us to school.

Immediately Adrian drove out of the school gates. I took off my school uniform shirt, making Adrian gasp, and the car swerved a little out of control before he got a firmer grip on the steering.

"What are you doing?" He asked.

"I'm changing duh, do you think I want to enter the station with my uniform?" I deadpanned. We weren't going to the hospital, and I didn't blame Adrian's mum for not telling the principal where exactly we were going because there was no need to explain why.

He shrugged and focused his attention on the road. I chuckled and quickly slipped on the white shirt I had kept in Adrian's car earlier, then put on my blue jeans first before taking off the skirt.

Shortly after we got to the station, Adrian took off his shirt, and I got down from the car so he could change his trousers, too. Even if we finished early from here, I didn't plan on returning to school.

Adrian got down from the car, now putting on black jeans instead of his uniform trousers and a white graphic T-shirt replacing his uniform shirt.

"Good morning, how may..." the lady behind the desk said before Adrian's mother cut her short.

"Adrian, Funke!" She called, and we all turned to look at her. She wore simple blue jeans and a green shirt with some words written on it I couldn't decipher.

We walked to where she was standing, and she led us to an interrogation room. She told me to sit and for Adrian to follow her, since it was just me they were going to interrogate at the moment. Shortly after, a female police officer walked into the room and sat down opposite me, the wooden table separating us.

"How are you today?" She asked.

"Good morning ma, I'm fine," I answered, my lips stretched in a thin line. Was I truly ready for this?

She pressed a button on the camera standing in front of her, which was already set up. It was like my life was a movie, being brought into an interrogation room and asked questions, the camera either in view or hidden.

The woman cleared her throat before speaking. She looked friendly. "What is your name?"

"Olufunke Ayodeji," I answered plainly.

"Do you know this man?" She pushed forward a picture of my stepfather.

"Yes, he's my stepfather," I swallowed the lump in my throat, I wasn't comfortable talking about my stepfather, especially with someone I didn't know but this was a necessity, I had to testify, I had to tell my story.

"Does he treat you well? Is he abusive?" She looked at me, making eye contact. I couldn't tell if she was being pitiful at the moment or just doing her job.

The flashes of my past and my stepfather's abuse came to my mind and I suddenly couldn't speak. My mouth felt dry. I closed my mouth and swallowed my saliva to moisten my throat. It wasn't working.

"Are you okay?" The lady asked. "Do you need water?"

I nodded wordlessly, and I watched her stand up and walk to the door, telling someone to get me water. A few seconds after, a bottle of water appeared on the table and the lady sat back down.

I quickly uncapped the bottle and gulped its content down as if my life depended on it. When satisfied, I recapped the bottle and spoke before my mouth could get dry again. "No, he doesn't treat me well. He is very abusive and…" I opened the water and drank again, feeling my mouth getting dry, "he's a rapist."

The lady nodded, "are you a firsthand victim, or yo–"

"He raped me," I voiced out stopping the woman from saying more. "Countless times. He has–" I focused my attention on the now empty bottle of water, "beaten me up, verbally abused me, and forced me to go for an abortion."

The lady's eyes widened, and she seemed taken aback by my confession. I was sure she wasn't expecting this. It was likely that when she heard about the case; she thought it was just some teenage spoilt child overreacting.

"When did all this start?" She asked, her voice sounding more serious than when we started.

"When I was eight, he used to beat me and insult me till I was twelve, then he started raping me," I answered.

"And what about your mother? Where was she when all this was happening?"

"She's always busy, on business trips, so she's never at home."

"Are you always home alone or is there someone or people who live with you at home, or do they come around regularly?" She was furiously writing on her notepad.

"The housekeeper and gateman. Ayanda is always around from about six in the morning to seven in the evening and the gateman is always around."

"Ayanda being the housekeeper, right?" She looked up at me and I nodded. She went back to her notes. "Does your father have friends or people who come around to visit often or once in a while?"

"He has friends, but I've never really met them personally. I'm mostly in my room when they come, just a few glances here and there."

"You said the housekeeper and gateman are around at a fair amount of time, so they must have noticed what was going on in the house, right?"

I was having a headache from the questions. "I do not know if they noticed because my stepfather is very careful."

"Have you ever spoken to anyone about it?"

"Yes, I told my best friend Adrian about the beatings and insults, but I never told him about the sexual abuse."

176

She gave me a confused look, "why didn't you?"

My head spun. "Because I was scared. He threatened that if I told anyone about what happened that he would kill me and my mother." My mind went back to the first night he made that threat and I shuddered.

"You mentioned he forced you to go for an abortion. How many times and what hospital?" She scrunched up her nose in obvious disgust.

I took in a deep breath. This was getting too much for me, "five times and at a private clinic not too far from the house, *Grace Clinic*."

She nodded as she wrote on her note, "thank you very much, that would be all for now. You're free to go."

With the pounding in my head increasing and my head spinning, I suddenly felt the urge to flush out the contents of my stomach. "Please, where is the restroom?"

"Down the hall to your left," she directed.

In a flash, I was on my feet and out of the room, running down the path she directed me. I could hardly see anything, just using my senses to get through. I passed Adrian and his mother on the way and they were saying something when they saw me, but I ignored them and pushed open the toilet door. I entered the first stall I saw and crouched over the toilet, sending the contents of my stomach out.

"Funke!" I heard Adrian yell as his voice got louder with every letter of my name.

I didn't respond as I held my stomach, unable to stop my body from flushing out my breakfast the same way it came in.

"Funke!" Adrian called again and his fists were pounding on the door of the stall I was in.

I flushed the toilet when the urge to puke had stopped and it felt like there was nothing left in my stomach. I stood up, opened the door, and rushed to the sink to rinse my mouth and splash water on my face.

"Funke are you alright?" Adrian asked, and I turned to him.

I nodded, "I'm fine."

"Come here," he pulled me to him and wrapped me in a comforting hug.

"It's going to be alright, I promise," he whispered as he stroked my hair.

I didn't have the strength to cry, I just wanted to curl up in a ball on my bed and sleep.

"Adrian, you're needed," his mother said as she walked into the restroom.

Adrian released me from his grip and left the restroom without another word. I looked at his mother and nodded to tell her I was okay.

She nodded and led us out of the restroom.

Lagos

Chapter Twenty Two

I had woken up very early that morning: a few minutes to five. I couldn't go back to sleep, so I went downstairs and get some work done in the house. With everything that was going on, I sued my stepfather so we were constantly going to court or meeting with my lawyer while preparing for SSCE (Senior School Certificate Examination) and UTME (Unified Tertiary Matriculation Examination) I never had time for myself not to talk about time to do anything meaningful in the house, like cooking or cleaning.

Though Adrian's mother had hired someone to do all of that in the house, a few times I felt bad that I wasn't able to do anything.

SAVING HER

After my stepfather was sued, my mother rushed down to Nigeria and canceled all of her business plans until further notice. I refused to go back to her house, so I had been staying with Adrian and his mum ever since. Not only did the house give me nightmares, but my mother and I weren't exactly the best of friends. She came to visit me regularly.

The kitchen was spotless when I stepped in, so I decided to make breakfast. Adrian's mum had a morning shift in the hospital, meaning she was going to be up soon.

Beans flour and pap were available, so I made *Akara* and *Pap* for breakfast. I made pap for just her and myself since Adrian was still sleeping.

She stepped into the kitchen just when I was done with cooking. I started cleaning the kitchen. "Good morning ma."

She looked around the kitchen and I could tell from her facial expression that she was shocked. She was wearing her nurse's uniform, and she held her handbag.

"You cooked," she finally said.

I laughed. "Yeah. I hope *Akara* and *Pap* are okay for breakfast."

"Why not?" She disappeared into the dining room before she appeared back in the kitchen. This time, she wasn't holding her handbag.

She served herself while I was still cleaning up the kitchen. When she finished serving herself, she went to the dining to eat.

I finished cleaning and served myself before joining her in the dining. "Is it okay?"

"It's great Funke, I didn't know you could cook like this." She said with a mouthful of food.

I sighed, happy that my food didn't taste like crap and I wasn't poisoning my best friend and his mother.

She finished eating before me, but it looked like she was waiting for me to finish eating before she stood up.

When I was finally done, I looked at her. "Aren't you going to work?"

"I am. I want to ask, where did you learn to cook? Was it your mum?" She was apprehensive while speaking, and I knew why.

Everyone knew the topic of my mother was to be slowly threaded upon; I didn't enjoy talking about her.

"She taught me a few things here and there, but I learned the majority through my housekeeper, Ayanda," I answered and stood up.

"Alright, thank you for the food. She took her handbag from the table. Make sure you and Adrian read today. Your exams are getting closer." She walked towards the front door.

"Yes ma, have a nice day at work." I cleared the plates.

Just when I finished washing the plates we used, Adrian walked into the kitchen.

"I knew I smelt food." He said groggily.

"Good morning." I wiped my hands dry with a napkin. "You can make *Pap* for yourself, right?" I laid the napkin on the kitchen counter.

"Yes." he wiped his face and ran his hand through his hair. "You cooked?" Like his mother, he was shocked to hear that I prepared breakfast.

"Yes. Enjoy, I'll be upstairs." The tip of my fingers lightly brushed his bicep as I walked past him.

At the foot of the stairs, I heard my phone ringing, and I realized I forgot it on the kitchen counter.

"Funke, you forgot your phone!" Adrian said after me and I rushed back into the kitchen.

"Who is calling?" I reached out for the said phone and Adrian handed it to me.

"Your lawyer." I was shocked to hear that. First, it was a little too early in the morning for her to be calling me.

I quickly answered the call, "hello?"

"Funke good morning I hope I didn't wake you up."

"No, you didn't. I was already awake. Hope no problems."

"I've been getting a lot of calls from journalists and media houses, all of them asking about your case. Do you want to make it public? I would have called earlier, but I didn't want to wake you up." She answered.

I put the call on speaker, getting Adrian's attention. "Sorry, come again."

She repeated herself, and Adrian and I shared a look. He shrugged, meaning the decision was all up to me.

"I want to keep it as private as possible, please." I finally answered.

"Alright, I'll do my best to stop the news from spreading. Have a nice day then."

"You too," I hung up.

"Are you sure you want to keep it private?" Adrian asked.

"Yes Adrian, I don't want people at school to look at me with pity or disgust. I'm tired of being the topic of discussion already." The last thing I needed was more attention from strangers than I was already getting.

It did not surprise me to find out that the news was slowly spreading. After all, Seyi had a prominent position while working at Shell. One reason he was always at home was because he preferred to work from home and they gave him that liberty. Immediately Shell heard the charges against him, they immediately fired him. I knew Shell was trying to avoid the news from spreading so fast, but word flies around with the speed of light these days with the aid of technology.

"You have a point." Adrian agreed with me.

"I'm going upstairs. Call me if you need me," I said and headed for the stairs.

I hadn't gotten halfway up the stairs before I heard Adrian shout my name, this time with more urgency. I rushed to the living room where he was.

He was standing by the window and looking outside. I stood beside him and my mouth dropped when I saw what he saw. There were journalists with their microphones and cameras. The gate was halfway open and I could see the gatekeeper trying to stop them from entering the house.

Without saying another word, Adrian took my phone and dialed my lawyer. I was beyond shocked at what I was seeing. I didn't know the news had spread so fast. How did they even find where I was staying?

"She said we should stay inside. She's on her way." Adrian dragged me away from the window and forced me to sit on the couch.

I was shaking with fear, fear that the entire world already knew my story and I couldn't keep my identity unknown. I didn't like the idea of my face being the headline of every newspaper and article

"Try not to think, okay? Your lawyer is handling everything." Adrian said to me as he sat beside me.

SAVING HER

I nodded and tried not to think because I knew thinking would lead to having a panic attack and that was the last thing I needed at that moment. About ten minutes after, my lawyer and my mother showed up at the house. After making sure that I was alright, she made calls and in two hours, the front of the house was empty. They had all gone.

I thanked her, and she stayed for about an hour to be sure none of them came back to the house or disturbed her or me with calls. She assured me that was going to be the last time it happened, but somehow I knew she was wrong and next time, it was going to be worse than this.

Lagos

Chapter Twenty Three

For the first time in a long time, my mother was around for a school event of mine. I was sure she was there because it was my secondary school graduation and she still felt bad about everything that happened with her husband, or should I say, almost ex-husband. She filed for a divorce.

So far, this was the only thing in my life I was ready to celebrate, since most of my life had been shitty. I was finally graduating from high school and getting free from its bondage. I was supposed to apply to a university and start getting ready for university life, but because of the case of my stepfather, I had to sit back for a year or even two. It was depressing seeing my mates move on with their lives and advance to the next stage, but this was something I had to deal with once and for all.

As I stared at myself in the mirror, I admired the dress I was wearing: an off-shoulder wine red dress that hugged my body perfectly, highlighting every single curve. It had a slit that ran up to my knee. For the dress, I had to take off the scarlet necklace that Adrian gave me and I left my neck bare. From the mirror, I could see my medals hanging on the far wall of my room and the trophy sitting on the table just underneath the medals. I had three medals, all gold. At least that was something else in my life I was oddly grateful for.

My room was almost empty, as I had packed up most of my clothes and personal things. Adrian, his mother, and my mother begged me to stay with my mother for about a week, which took a lot of convincing. We hardly spoke to each other, just a few words here and there. It was the definition of awkward. After my one week with my mother, I would go back to staying at Adrian's place for as long as I can. Staying in this house still gave me nightmares and the feeling of dread, as if my stepfather were here.

I picked my purse from my vanity just beside the mirror and I walked out of the room, my heels clicking on the tiled floor. I was walking freely around the house because my stepfather was now behind bars, temporarily, and we were hoping it would be permanent or at least for many years to come. The fact remained that I had peace of mind and that was something for someone that hadn't had it in years.

"I'm ready," I called to my mum as I got downstairs.

"Let's go," she got up from the couch and I followed her out of the house. She stopped me from walking and helped me fix a braid that was hanging loosely at the side of my head.

"Thanks." We got into the car and she drove off.

"I'm so proud of you, Funke," Mum said to me as she drove.

I smiled. "Thank you, mum."

I met with Adrian in the parking lot and we walked into the school hall and took our seats. His mum was still at work, so it was only him for now.

The event went on and I was bored throughout. The juniors sang a farewell song for us and that was the only time that I didn't feel like sleeping. As much as I hated school and the fact that they forced me to have some social interactions, it was fair to say that I would miss school. Though I was always quiet and in the shadows, I was always attentive, especially to certain details. Because I hardly spoke in class, people always made the mistake of discussing some very juicy topics around me, thinking that I wouldn't talk to anyone or spill their secrets. Well, I always did a lot of talking to Adrian and I was going to miss that.

Because of everything going on, I hadn't had the chance to think about going to the university, but I had one school in mind, the University of Ibadan. I hoped I could go there someday.

When the event ended, I was exhausted. First from wearing heels for so long and second from standing up a good number of times when the majority still sat: When they were giving awards, I won an award for best graduating student and best in English. Then when we walked to get our certificates, it was a long walk.

I was ready to leave but Adrian wasn't, so he told me to wait for him in front of our classroom-sorry old classroom-that he was going to be quick.

My phone beeped with a new notification from Instagram. Someone tagged me in a post. I opened the post, realizing it was our class's official Instagram page. They posted the group picture we recently took, and I didn't know how, but they got my handle and tagged me in it. I wanted to un-tag myself but I left it, for future sake.

I heard voices coming toward me and I didn't need to look up before I knew they were talking about me.

"She's the one from that case I told you about." One girl said.

"What case?" The other one asked.

"The one about her stepfather sexually and physically abusing her. My father is friends with the judge. The news has slowly been spreading, but it's like they're trying to bring it down." The first girl replied.

"If I were her, I wouldn't want anyone to know, too." Their footsteps got closer and this time I looked up from my phone.

SAVING HER

I glared at the girls, and they both hastened their steps and ran away. I knew my mother and my lawyer were doing their best to keep the news from flying around, but there would be a few cracks here and there.

Adrian finally walked out of the classroom with a sour look on his face. He draped his hand over my waist and at that moment I turned around and instantly knew why his mood changed. Jasmine was standing in front of the class with a downcast look and when her eyes shifted to Adrian and I's retreating figures, her face shifted to anger.

I looked at Adrian again just as we rounded the corner and began going down the stairs. "What happened?" I asked.

"Nothing." He didn't look at me and his steps didn't falter for a second.

I waited till we were by my mother's car before I spoke again. "What happened Adrian?" This time, my voice was more demanding.

He sighed and opened the passenger's door of my mother's car for me. "It's nothing." He avoided my gaze.

I held his wrist and dragged him with me to the other side of the parking lot that had fewer people. "Talk to me, Adrian."

He tugged at his hair, messing it up even more. "She tried to kiss me."

He knew I knew who he was talking about. "Go on," I urged.

"When I refused, she asked if it was because of you, and when I said yes, she started lashing out about you, calling you name. She even had the guts to bring up your stepfather's case."

"And what did you say?"

"I warned her not to speak about you like that again." He paused and looked at me.

There was still more to say, but he wasn't saying anything.

I groaned. "For fuck's sake, just tell me!"

"Fine, she said that I'll never find love with someone as damaged as you," he looked away completely.

I didn't know what got into my head, but at that moment, I wanted to get on my tip-toes and kiss him. I didn't care what Jasmine had to say about me or what she thought about Adrian and me because I agreed with her. Adrian could never find love with someone like me, someone damaged. All I could think of at that moment was the fact that our reality troubled him: the reality of finding love with someone like me which implied that he saw a future with me, he saw himself falling in love with me and he had feelings for me. For a damaged girl, that was all I could think of at that moment: that the one person I had feelings for reciprocated them. The one question here was: was he willing to be with someone as damaged as me? That was the one thing I feared.

Before I could act on my thoughts, we both heard his name, and we both turned to look for the source of the voice, which was his mother. She was standing by her car with her arms crossed and a neutral expression on her face. My mum got out of her car she parked right beside Adrian's mother's car. She looked at all three of us, wondering what was going on.

Adrian turned to me and planted a kiss on my cheek. "Congratulations." He said and stepped back with a smile on his face.

I greeted his mum before getting into my mother's car. Adrian's mood swings were always giving me a whiplash.

"Is everything okay?" Mum got into the car and started the engine.

"Yeah," I wore my seatbelt.

"Are you sure?" She asked, her eyes on landing me for a second.

"Yeah." The last thing I wanted was for my mother to be in on my business.

I guessed it was going to take a long while for me to open up to her. It took a while for me to open up to Adrian, who was always there for me, talk less of my mum, who had been absent for almost all of my life.

She sighed heavily but remained quiet the entire drive home.

Hours after, mum called me downstairs for dinner. I picked up my phone from my nightstand, where I plugged it and headed downstairs. As I went down the stairs, I was looking at my notifications. I was tagged in a bunch of Instagram and Facebook stories and posts. I had a bunch of new followers and DMs that I wasn't ready to look at or respond to. I locked the phone just as I got to the living room and tucked it into the back pocket of my skirt.

Mum wasn't at the dining table but the table was set, so I took my food and went to the living room to eat. I found mum standing close to the TV screen with the remote in her hand and a frown on her face.

"What are you watching?" I looked at the TV this time and I dropped everything I was holding. The plate shattered into a million pieces on the floor and the hot food spilled all over my legs and onto the floor.

Mum turned around. A yelp escaped her lips and her hand clutched at her chest.

"Shit," she said, looking at me, then the spilled food, and then back at the TV. She turned it off.

Without caring that I was probably going to get myself injured, I marched to her and took the remote from her hand, switching the TV back on.

My face was on the TV screen and the news reporter was going on about me and the fact that I just graduated from secondary school. The group picture I and my classmates took showed on the screen. Unlike my

SOFIIA DAVIID

classmates, they revealed my face while that of my classmates were blurred.

What I had been running away from was happening and for the second time.

"Funke, calm down," Mum said and took out her phone from her pocket and started dialing whoever it was.

I couldn't get to hear her side of the conversation because she walked out the front door just as my phone started ringing. I wanted to ignore it, but I saw it was Adrian, so I answered the call. My mind was blank, so I couldn't say anything. Nothing made sense anymore.

"Funke?" Adrian called, but I remained silent, my head trying to figure out what to tell him. "I can hear you breathing. What's going on?" His voice was laced with panic, and I heard shuffling in the background. "Okay, just stay where you are. I'm on my way." I expected him to hang up, but he didn't.

I crawled to the corner of the living room and sat on the floor. I held my knees to my chest, desperately trying not to have a panic attack. Adrian kept talking to me and assuring me he was on his way.

SAVING HER

This day officially joined the list of the 'worst days of my life.' A day that was supposed to bring me joy and happiness, but no, life decided that it wasn't done playing with me, so it found a way to spread my news and my face all over the TV for the world to see.

At a point, I knew Adrian was talking, but I couldn't wrap my head around whatever he was saying. All I could hear was his words merging to one and reaching my ears as gibberish.

Mum and Adrian ran into the house and they were both by my side in an instant, fear written all over their faces. As I stared into space, my body rocked back and forth. I couldn't hear what they were saying. My plan to not have a panic attack was definitely not working. I could feel the breath in my lungs slowly vanish and I could feel my hands shaking, then slowly working its way up the rest of my body.

Adrian drew me to him, so I was resting between his legs as he sat on the floor. He held my palms together and kept whispering 'breathe' in my ear.

I closed my eyes and did as I was told. It was slowly taking effect. My breathing slowly normalized, and the shaking stopped. When I opened my eyes again, I was staring at Adrian's brown eyes. They held so much fear and uncertainty in them, but his hold on me didn't falter.

A while back, I had a panic attack in my bathroom and that was when I made research. Anything that might trigger those horrid memories in my head was bound to get me shaking and gasping for breath. After that day, I prayed to not have one again, but it just felt like all my prayers were falling on deaf ears.

I knew God was up there and that was why I didn't mean that statement literally. Growing up in a Nigerian home, belonging to a particular religion was a must and if you didn't belong to any, let's just say people wouldn't look at you the same way. I went to church every Sunday. If mum was around all three of us would go together but if mum wasn't around, most of the time I went by myself, which was the best for me, that way I wouldn't have had to deal with my stepfather's unnecessary shouts and rants.

I prayed and no; I had not given up on God because I knew he was up there and He always showed up for his children, but the thing was, sometimes your faith would go weak and you go faint in the spirit, that was what I was feeling at that moment. I hoped and a large part of me believed that one day I was going to get past all these but it felt too far away and sometimes it felt like it would not happen.

I kept holding on and my biggest prayer was that I didn't tire of holding on.

"Funke, can you hear me?" Adrian's panic-streaked voice reached my ears, and I broke out of my reverie.

"Yeah, I'm fine," I whispered, and held his shirt tighter.

Lagos

Chapter Twenty Four

I woke up with a start and the first thing I noticed was the cold sweat on my body, the air condition in my room was on, so the reason for my sweating was the horrible flashback I had as a dream. It felt so real, my stepfather calling me to his room and the usual happening.

I stood up from the bed and walked into the bathroom to splash some water on my face. I stopped for a second to stare at myself and I instantly regretted it. It was a reminder of who I was, what I had gone through, and how much I hated myself.

The bruise on my cheek had healed, but I felt the pain once again, so I reached out to touch my cheek. My left arm still had the cast on it, but was healing quickly. I noticed the scars on my hand and my shoulder. They were faint and almost invisible, but only if you knew where they were and looked hard would you find them.

I tore my gaze from the mirror and reached out to my medicine cabinet just above my head. I'm sure I had a razor somewhere. Finally finding it, I unwrapped it and stared at it.

The only way to get rid of this pain is to end my life. The razor was sharp, so I slowly placed it on my skin and just as I was about to apply some pressure, I heard my name and that startled me, making me drop the razor in my hand.

The door flung open and a confused Adrian stared back at me. He looked at me from head to toe and when his eyes landed on the razor on the floor, they widened and he rushed to my side. He pushed me out of the bathroom and into my room to sit on my bed.

He took my wrist in his hand to examine it for any marks. When he saw nothing, he looked at me with fear in his eyes. For the first time since I'd known Adrian, he looked speechless.

"What are you doing here?" I asked. "It's probably the middle of the night. What are you doing in my room?"

"I just couldn't sleep and I had this strong feeling to check on you and after much arguments with myself, I got up and came here. You didn't answer when I knocked so I let myself in scared that something was wrong, when I didn't see you in here I got more worried and came straight to your bathroom, when I knocked and you didn't answer again, it confirmed it that something was wrong," he paused. "I'm glad I came here. What were you thinking?" His eyes searched mine, trying to find an answer to all this.

"It is better I leave," I told him and looked away. He wasn't supposed to find me until all that was left of me was a cold and lifeless body.

He bit his lip and closed his eyes for a second. "I knew it, I just knew it."

I looked back at him, confused. "You knew what?"

"I think you're suffering from PTSD," he said, but that didn't help answer my question, only confused me more.

I gave him a look that said he should start explaining and he spoke, "PTSD, Post Traumatic Stress Disorder is an aftermath of traumatic events just like the name. And one of its many symptoms or should I call it side effects is suicidal thoughts and possible suicide attempts. I guessed that it could happen to you but I refused to dwell on that thought."

"I have nothing like that. Nothing is wrong with me. I just need to leave so all this pain would stop." I whisper yelled.

He shook his head, "come on." He helped me to stand up from the bed and led me out of my room.

He took me to the parlor upstairs and told me to sit down before taking out his phone from the pocket of his pajamas. We were currently at my house and Adrian agreed to the night here. The case is now bigger than I imagined. I've visited the courtroom more than I expected in the last months, but according to my lawyer, we were winning the case. We had to. The housekeeper, the gateman, Adrian, my mother and a few of Seyi's friends had testified against him when they were interrogated both in the court and outside now it's left for the court to decide his fate which was taking longer than I expected.

I was back in this house because it was Adrian, his mum, and my mum's silly attempt to get me closer to my mum. I only agreed to be here if Adrian was with me.

"Mum, we need you," Adrian said with his phone pressed to his ear.

I sank into the couch. I knew what was coming next.

I hated hospitals, not only because my stepfather had forced me to visit one on multiple occasions, but because of the smell and the gloom that lingered around them. This was a private hospital, but all hospitals were the same.

Adrian's mother concluded that it would be great if I went for a checkup after last night. Not just a mental checkup, but general too. We needed to know if everything about me was damaged or if it was just my brain. I still refused to believe that I had PTSD, as Adrian had said.

"Nurse Parker," the door of the room opened and we all looked at the doctor that walked in.

I had done an MRI scan and various blood tests, and now we all sat and waited for my fate in the hospital room. Adrian was sitting with me on the bed, my hand in his, and he squeezed it slightly for assurance.

The doctor went to the monitor in front of us, and a screen appeared. What I assumed was the result of the MRI scan was on display.

"Your body looks normal, your hand is healing properly, and physically, you're fine. Psychologically, you would have to see Doctor Andrew for that. Now there is something that I'd like to discuss with the patient alone."

They all murmured a quick 'okay' and soon they were all out of the room. The doctor occupied the chair my mum sat on seconds ago.

The screen of the monitor changed and what appeared to be a scan of a pregnant woman appeared. A pregnant woman? Why was he showing me this? I looked at the doctor, hoping he would explain because I was confused. He looked lost for words, like he was waiting for me to piece everything together, scared of how to break the news to me.

I looked at the scan again and I saw what looked like a fetus. It looked small, like something four or five weeks old. I had no medical knowledge, so I couldn't tell.

Wait, is this...? It couldn't be. *Have I seen my period for the month?*

No, I haven't and it's way past the usual time. I didn't even see my period last month, but I thought it was just the stress of the court cases and all that.

Not this again.

"It appears that you are eight weeks pregnant," the doctor said, confirming my thoughts.

All the images of me vomiting in the morning these past weeks, nausea, my breasts feeling a lot heavier than usual, and the slight irritation once in a while.

"I take it as you weren't aware." The doctor had this look of pity in his eyes. "Do you want to inform your parents about this yourself, or do I do it for you?"

I was speechless. My entire world had crashed right in front of me and I couldn't do anything about it.

"I can't do it," I said.

He nodded and stood up, then told everyone to come in. They all took their previous positions in the room and he started speaking. I couldn't hear anything but the loud ringing in my ears.

When the doctor finished speaking, he excused himself and I could finally hear again. Adrian stood up from beside me and stormed out of the room. He was angry.

I was once again pregnant for my stepfather and anyone deserved to be angry about it. The Doctor who helped me with my last abortion told me discretely that I should try not to come for a sixth abortion because the more I do it, the more my chances of having kids in the future reduces.

This was crazy. I felt like I was going crazy. My mother was the next to leave the room, her sobs getting louder.

Adrian's mother, who was beside me, pulled me in for a hug. "It'll be alright, you're going to be fine." She whispered into my ears.

I was tired of listening to their lies. *I will not be alright and neither will I be fine.*

I didn't know how long we sat down in the room but shortly after Adrian and my mother returned to the room, my mother kept apologizing to me but I didn't hear what she was saying. Adrian was silent throughout.

Doctor Andrew came in later and confirmed my PTSD. He noticed the gloominess in the room so he quickly left, telling us he would contact us to know if I'd want the therapy and if I didn't want it, what drugs I could take to and what to do on a day-to-day basis to help.

"I want an abortion," I announced, getting everyone's attention.

"What?" My mother's eyes widened.

"I want an abortion," I repeated, this time louder.

"You can't just have an abortion. You've had one five times, and having another one is like killing your future. Having kids may be difficult for you when you finally decide to get married and settle down." My mother spoke, but I wasn't having it.

"I can *just* get an abortion and you can't stop me, I'm eighteen now, plus even if I can't have kids in the future I don't care, I'm not carrying that bastard's baby in me and I don't want to be a shitty mother like you," I spat and my mother gasped.

"Alright, that's enough you two." Adrian's mother said, this time stopping the quarrel that was sure to break soon. "Funke, if you want an abortion, we will not stop you but I will tell you that your mother is right, getting another abortion will reduce your chances of having kids in the future so if you are getting one, think about it well. I don't want you carrying that man's child, but if it means saving your future, we can only pray for God's mercy and help."

I nodded, understanding what she was saying.

She spoke again, "also if you decide on getting an abortion, then at least let us get a DNA test now that we can. That will serve as another evidence in court."

I nodded once again.

"Can we get out of this place and please not another word about abortion? I beg you, at least not in front of me." Adrian stood up and walked out of the room. Shortly after, we all left the room.

Chicago

Chapter Twenty Five

"Adrian, have you seen my phone?" I ask from the living room. He is in the kitchen. I've been searching for my phone since we got back from work. I can't recall where I dropped it.

"It's here," Adrian says, and I heave a sigh of relief.

I rush into the kitchen and find it sitting on the counter. "Thanks."

My phone beeps with a new text and it of my mum telling me she just arrived in New Zealand. I scoffed. She could have called instead.

"What is it?" Adrian asks on seeing my facial expression.

"My mum, she just got to New Zealand," I tell him.

"Hmm, nice." His attention shifts back to the sandwich he is making, and I unconsciously lick my lips. They look delicious. He hands me a plate of the sandwich and I thank him before stuffing my mouth with it. I hear him chuckle, but I ignore him.

"Lucy is inviting us to a party with her tomorrow night."

A party. Do I want to go to one again? The first time wasn't too gratifying, but I think I want to take another shot at it. Lucy will be there, so I hopefully won't be stuck with Adrian all night.

"Alright." I lick my hands, done with the sandwich.

"Okay, I'll let her know you're on board," he takes out his phone from his pocket and starts typing. Seconds after, he tucks the phone back into the pocket of his trousers and takes a bite of his sandwich. "What college do you want to apply to?" He sits down on the stool beside me..

"Before all that happened, I always wanted to go to UI." I answer. UI, University of Ibadan. A very competitive school but our grades are good enough to let us in. I nod, "what do you want to think?"

"It's a good school." He shrugs.

"You still down to study theatre arts?" I remember when we were still in secondary school and Adrian would go on and on about his dreams of studying theatre arts and how he prayed to one day make it big in the movie industry.

He nods. "What about you, still down to study –" he pauses to think. "What's that weird course again?"

I playfully push him and he laughs. He always found my dream course of study weird, though it wasn't for me. "European studies," I tell him. "I don't intend to staying in Nigeria forever," I say. "And no, I won't rely on my mother for that again. The next time I'll be leaving Nigeria will be because of my hard work and not because my mother wants to favor me."

"She's not favoring you, just trying to make up for the past." he shakes his head, disagreeing with me.

I'm not having it. "She knows I don't like her, so she's trying to make me like her again." I argue.

He sighs. "I will not argue with you." He waves a dismissive hand. "We need to prepare ourselves for JAMB again."

"JAMB," I groan. The exam that makes every Nigerian student almost lose their shit. "Please, no extra lessons. We study together," I plead.

"Are you sure? It's been almost two years,"

"I'm sure. We can do this together. I don't need some teacher who believes they are better than us." I reach for his hand.

"Alright," he gives my hand a reassuring squeeze, "together."

JAMB, Joint Admission Matriculation Board was the board that conducted the exam UTME (Unified Tertiary Matriculation Examination). Everyone refers to the exam as JAMB, so we just go with it. UTME is written in one day, but the pressure the world puts on you makes you feel like the exam is going to go on for days. It's an exam that determines who you are and become. If your score is low, you're seen as a failure. If your score is high, you're seen as very intelligent and if your score is somewhere in the middle, you need to step up your game or in their terms, *'you could have done better.'*

In my opinion, who I get to be in the future shouldn't be determined by one stupid exam. What if I'm not meant

215

to go to college? What if I don't want to go to college? If I fail the exam, that doesn't mean I'm a failure. It may mean I just need to try harder, and it may mean that isn't what I'm supposed to do. Don't get me wrong, exams are necessary, but that doesn't mean that one exam gets to define who I am. This is something that every Nigerian parent and the Nigerian society needs to know. But I think they are gradually coming to terms with that.

At this moment, it feels like it is me and Adrian against the world, just us. I hope things turn out the way I want them to.

Adrian and I are currently shopping online for the books we would need for our upcoming exam. Registration doesn't start until February and that will need us to be in

Nigeria then and when it is time to write the exam. We will also write our UTME in Nigeria and after writing it, our vacation will officially be over.

Now that I think about it, maybe I should just sit back here and study here instead. It won't be a problem for Adrian and neither would it be one for me. My mum is rich. All we need to do is write the SATs and apply to a university and hope to enter.

Deep, deep down, studying at UI has always been a dream of mine since I was little and even up to a few years ago, the bullshit going on in my life made me give up on the dream but I guess it's not too late to pick it back up.

"Do you want to study at UI or you're just doing this because of me?" The guilt is settling in my chest that his suffering to go back to Nigeria is because of me.

He takes his eyes from his laptop and sets them on me. "No, I want to do this on my own. UI is an elite school, recognized globally, so if I still change my mind later on I can. Plus, if I don't come with you, who will take care of you? I know you're a grown-up, but you still need someone there for familiarity and I'm a no better person for the job."

He's right, I need him. I can't imagine being on that big campus all alone. I doubt I will make friends that quick or make any friends at all. I'll probably ask to be transferred to whatever school Adrian is in or to school online. I'll be dammed.

I give him a small smile and he smiles back, "I'll keep saying this: I'll always be here for you."

"Thanks for being here." I fight the tears threatening to spill.

I value this friendship more than anything and I won't trade it for the world.

We got a few necessary books and past questions. After we had a video call with Adrian's mum also, she told us she would come over to visit soon. She looked good and I can't wait to see her. She is one of the good things that went right in my life.

Lagos

Chapter Twenty Six

My hands involuntarily went to the baby bump that had slowly been increasing lately. If I wore the right clothes, from a distance you wouldn't know until I got closer to you.

Adrian and I originally planned to leave the country to Chicago after high school, but when my case was taken to court, we knew we still had a long way to go, Nigeria, and its wonderful turn of events.

My mum had been thinking of sending me and Adrian to a small town where I could avoid unwanted attention from my teenage pregnancy and take a little breath of fresh air, but just like the Chicago situation, I couldn't go anywhere; I needed to be in court a few times.

It was still hard to come to the fact that I would be having a baby for my stepfather. I wouldn't lie. I already hated the baby because of the father, but I knew I had to be the best mother I could ever be for my child. My mother made a lot of mistakes and I didn't plan on doing the same thing.

I quickly tied a band around my hair and took one last long look at my face in the mirror before heading out the door. I could barely recognize myself anymore: I had put on so much weight and I was sure I looked so ugly by now. We were supposed to have lunch together at *Rodina's*, Adrian, his mum, my mum and I. My mum was already waiting at the front door for me, so she took my hand and led us to the car. She hates my pregnancy, but everyone knew that if I lost this pregnancy, my life and future were at stake. They had all been treating me like an egg since we got the news three months ago, making sure that I was fine.

After my mother married my stepfather when I was eight, she never tried having another child. According to her, she never wanted more than one child and she was content with me. We all knew that it was because of her busy schedule: she couldn't sit in one place and cater to a baby. She would lose her mind.

We could now see the restaurant a few blocks ahead and shortly after, my mother was parking the car just beside Adrian's. We got into the building and Adrian and his mother were the first people I noticed. Adrian's mum was still in her scrubs, obviously just leaving the hospital for her lunch break.

We went over and I sat down beside Adrian. "Hey."

"How are you?" He beamed at me.

"I'm okay, I guess." I shrugged. "Good afternoon ma," I greeted his mum.

"How are you today, Funke?" She smiled.

"I'm okay," I forced a smile.

Thinking about it, I realized I wasn't feeling okay at that moment. My head felt light, like I was going to fall anytime. I looked at Adrian and he was saying something, but I couldn't hear the words that left his lips. I looked down at the floor by my feet and the last thing I saw before the darkness took over was blood on the white tiles.

"Is she awake?" I barely heard someone say. Not just someone, Adrian, I could recognize that voice anywhere and anytime.

"I think so," this voice was clearer now, my mum.

I forced my eyes open and all I saw was a white wall. Adrian was smiling at me when I turned to my left. I turned to my right and my mum was doing the same.

What is going on?

"How are you feeling?" Adrian asked.

I tried to sit up and Adrian helped me, "confused, what is going on?"

He gave my mother a look before returning his gaze to me. "You lost the baby, a miscarriage."

I didn't know if I should cry or jump for joy. I no longer carried the child of a rapist, an unwanted child, I was free from that burden and I couldn't be happier, but this was a child, a child that I would have grown to love despite my absolute resentment for its father. A soul was lost, and I didn't have the tears to cry over it. *Does that make me a bad person?*

The door flew open and Adrian's mum and the doctor from when I first had the scan; I think his name was Dr. Segun, walked into the room, they were talking in hushed whispers and were oblivious to the fact that I was now awake.

"What are you two yapping about?" Mum's words got their attention.

"It's–" Aunt Dianne stopped talking when she noticed I was awake. "Oh, Funke you're awake." She rushed to my side. "How are you feeling?"

I nodded. "I feel fine."

"Nice to see you again, miss, though I was hoping for a better situation," the doctor gave me a tight smile. He pressed a few things on the tablet in his hands. "You lost the baby and you're fortunately in a good shape. We'd

223

conduct a test tomorrow to be sure that there are no lying complications that we might have missed earlier. Apart from that, with exercise, good food and sufficient rest, you'll be up and running like before."

"Will I be able to have a child again?" I still wanted the opportunity to have a child that I want and planned for.

He sighed, "to our greatest surprise, your womb is in good shape despite all the troubles it has been through so yes, you can still have a baby if you want but you'll need medical scrutiny through the journey just to be sure that your life will not be at risk in any way."

I heaved a sigh of relief. At least I still had a chance at being a decent mother, and that was all that mattered to me at that moment.

Chapter Twenty Seven

The doorbell rings 1 so I stand up to answer the door. We are expecting Adrian's mum, so I don't bother looking through the peephole before opening the door. It has been two weeks since our video call and last night she confirmed she was flying in today.

I was smiling, something I hardly do, but upon seeing a stranger who was not Adrian's mum or a delivery guy from anywhere, the smile fades.

"Good afternoon. How may I help you?" We got back from work less than thirty minutes ago and Adrian ran upstairs to take a shower and he hasn't come downstairs ever since.

"Does Adrian Parker live here?" His voice sends shivers down my spine. Not in a good way.

I try not to hide my fear as I clear my throat, silently praying for Adrian to appear behind me, freshly showered. How long does it take to shower?

"Um, who's asking?" I hope my stalling skills are working.

"Me, I'm his–"

"Dad?" Adrian says from behind me, cutting the man short from his sentence.

Wait, did Adrian finish that sentence for him? Did he say 'dad'?

I am both relieved and confused at the same time. What is going on here?

Adrian never spoke about his father. That was his unspoken rule and I respected it. According to him, his father left him and his mum when he was five and that was the main reason his mum left their lives in America and moved to Nigeria. That was the reason Adrian ended up in that wonderful place. If not for his father, who is magically in front of me, he wouldn't go through all he went through. But if he never got to Nigeria, we wouldn't have met and I probably would still be under the torments of my stepfather. Everything happens for a reason, all things work together for my good.

"Son," the man's face softens upon seeing Adrian.

"Don't call me that, I made a mistake calling you *dad* just now," Adrian comes closer to where I'm standing. "What are you doing here?"

His father's face drops on hearing Adrian's word, "I heard you were in town so I thought I'd drop by and…" He takes in a deep breath, "I just thought that I could get to see you. It's been years since we last saw."

"Now you've seen me, get out." Adrian doesn't blink as those words leave his mouth.

"Adrian," I hiss. He's being a little too harsh.

"Don't give me that, Funke. You're no better than me."

I take a step backward. He is right, I'm no better than him. The sight of my mum puts me on the edge all the time, and this is no different. I shouldn't be telling him how to speak to his father.

"Sorry." I drop my head and begin walking back into the house, but Adrian stops me.

"Wait, I'm sorry," he grips my right arm.

"No, you're right. I shouldn't get to tell you how to speak to your father. After all, I'm no better than you." I shrug.

He opens his mouth to speak again, but his mother's voice stops him.

"What are you doing here?" She asks his father as she takes the last step up the front porch.

"Destiny," his father smiles.

"Answer the question George, what are you doing here?" I've never seen his mum this serious before. She had a scowl on her face.

"I came to see my son. That's the least you can let me do after five years."

Adrian came over for a quick visit five years ago and he ran into his dad. It was the last time he laid eyes on his father. His father still lived in town.

"You stopped being his father the day you walked out of his life, so get out of here before I call the cops on you for trespassing," his mum orders.

I am starting to feel like the third wheel. I'm just a bystander, unwanted. I should probably leave and let them settle their issue.

228

As I turn around to leave, Adrian pulls me back, just like earlier. "Where are you going?"

"To give you space." I say.

"Please stay, I need you." He whispers.

I nod and stand as I did before. Adrian needs me, so I'll be there for him.

"Destiny,please–"

"Leave," Adrian's mum orders again, this time louder.

The man nods and takes out a card from his wallet and hands it to Adrian. He collects the card slowly, a look of confusion on his face.

"Call me if you ever change your mind," and with that, he turns around and walks away.

We all stand by the door till his retreating figure is now out of sight. I'm the first to head inside the house, pulling Adrian with me.

"I'm sorry about that Funke, how are you?" Adrian's mum says as she closes the door behind her.

"I'm fine. How was your flight?" I take her bag, which is lighter than I imagined.

"It was okay. I'm hungry. What's there to eat?" She ruffles Adrian's hair, "are you okay?"

"There's *Jollof* Spag and cereal," I shrug. "Adrian and I need to go grocery shopping."

She is about to speak but holds her tongue when Adrian stomps upstairs. She sighs and takes out her purse, giving me her credit card. "You guys should go shopping together. I have a headache and he can be a bit difficult sometimes." She sits on the couch, closing her eyes.

"Alright." I know what she meant: I should help calm her son down. I agree with her, Adrian can be a bit difficult sometimes.

When upstairs, I first drop her bag in the guest room before heading to Adrian's room to look for him. He is sitting on his bed, his elbows resting on his knees and his palms cupping his cheeks.

He looks up when I walk in, "hey."

"Get up, we're going grocery shopping." I drag him by his left arm and pull him out of the room and downstairs. He doesn't complain.

I took the car keys from the coffee table. My therapist saw it as a great idea to get a driver's license so my movements wouldn't be restricted. I got it last week. Though I have a few more months to be here, I don't mind.

The silence during the drive to the store is deafening, and the radio isn't doing a good job. When Adrian is in *this* mood, I have to choose my words carefully; the last thing I need is to hit a wrong nerve. I am just coming up with the right words when I pull over at the store, so I seal my lips. We go in and take a cart, ready to shop.

"Should I call him?" Adrian asks, throwing in a carton of fruit loops. I don't like that cereal.

"It's your choice. Do you want to?" I add the milk to our cart.

"I think so. There is a part of me that needs my father. I never had one and he's willing to be one so," he stops walking for a second. "It's just so hard to let go."

"That makes two of us." my voice is low, but Adrian hears me and chuckles. "I get it, take your time to think about it, it's always your choice," I shrug.

Some girls at the other end of the aisle are staring at Adrian and whispering amongst themselves. Adrian notices them and the blonde girl sends him a wave to which he waves back, forcing a smile just for them.

I'm sorry girls, you don't have a chance at all. I hurriedly shove the things we need on that aisle into the cart before dragging Adrian together with the cart away from there.

I don't know this new feeling, but it's not good.

"Okay, let's make a deal," Adrian proposes and I stopped walking.

"What deal?"

"If I call my dad and probably meet up with him. You'll have a heart-to-heart talk to your mum and this time, you do most of the talking.," he folds his arms across his chest.

I shake my head, "no, no, that's not fair."

"Come on, please for me." He pleads, jutting out his bottom lip.

I look away. I'm not falling for the puppy look. "No Adrian, no," I walk ahead of him.

"Please Funke, please," he is now in front of me.

I sigh, "Fine." It won't kill me. After all, she may not pick up the call. She's in New Zealand.

Thank you."

I hum in response.

SAVING HER

He is looking brighter than when we stepped in, like the Adrian I know.

At the farthest end of the aisle, I notice the same girl I saw a few weeks ago at the cinema, but she isn't with her boyfriend. She's with an older woman I guess is her mother.

They are walking toward the other aisle so they don't see me. The girl is wearing plain blue jeans, and a top made of Ankara with white sneakers. She looks good and I admire her from here till they disappear from my sight.

Adrian and I continue our shopping and not long after we are back home. We prepare dinner and I'm soon cuddling my pillow on the couch, my eyes on the TV.

Chapter Twenty Eight

The judge's last words resounded in my ears. The fight was over, my stepfather was sentenced to jail and justice was served. It had been an entire year of this bumpy road, a broken arm, and bruises, pregnancy, a miscarriage, and a PTSD diagnosis, but it was finally over. PTSD exempted. I wasn't sure if I was ready to face it.

"Funke, it is over," Adrian whispered, causing a smile to form on my face.

We stood up at the same time and walked to my mother's car, our mother's walking behind us. We got into the car without saying another word.

"So, where should we go to celebrate?" Adrian's mother asked when we were all buckled up.

They all yelled various joints and I remained quiet till their voices had died down.

"How about we go home, have a drink, order some pizza, watch a movie and probably have a dive in the pool?" I suggested.

"Sounds great, less money to spend," Adrian reasoned.

"You're not having a dive in the pool. We're in the rainy season," Adrian's mum pointed out.

"Almost raining season," my mum piped in, surprising me by supporting Ame and Adrian.

"Dianne, you support them," Adrian's mum was shocked, too.

"Destiny, they're just kids. Let them enjoy the peak of their youth," she shocked me once again.

"We are not kids," Adrian said and I agreed with him.

"Oh please," my mum waved us off and we laughed.

I was the first one to enter my house. Some papers on the coffee table made me stop in my tracks. They were divorce papers.

Because of my ongoing case, she just recently got the full process of the divorce ongoing. They had both appended their signatures at the bottom of the paper and I sighed in relief. Now I have nothing to do with that man.

My mum came up beside me, and when she saw the papers in my hand, she took them from me and gave me a small smile before pulling me in for a hug. Though I had a little resentment towards her, she was still my mother.

Adrian and his mum walked into the house laughing and when they saw us hugging each other, they joined in on the hug, I may not have a real family but these people were my family, blood-related or not, one thing was binding us together, love.

I wouldn't be here now if it wasn't for them. I would be in a classroom at the university, scared to go home because I knew what was going to happen if I did. I wouldn't have been able to write my WASSCE (West African Senior School Examination) and passed as I did. Adrian and I took the exam shortly after I told him what was going on and some police officers became my friends.

It was tough considering what was going on, but we still passed the exams. We'd be heading to Chicago in a week from now and after our break there, Adrian and I would come back to Nigeria to study. Studying in Nigerian Federal universities was always a drag because of their weird ways of making students suffer, but I didn't mind it. I was a Nigerian after all, plus it was something Adrian and I had agreed on.

To say the thought didn't scare me would be a lie. I feared what might become of me. I was scared shitless, mainly because of my PTSD, but I was also ready for whatever was coming at me. It was a change and I was learning to embrace it.

Chicago

Chapter Twenty Nine

I will always be there for Adrian and that is why when he asked me to go with him to see his dad, I agreed, even though I'll be the third wheel.

The café isn't too far from the house, so we were there in record time. We took the seats close to the exit, getting a good view of the city. Schools had resumed, so there weren't many teenagers and young adults around. When Lucy invited us to a party this Friday, I was shocked because she's supposed to be back in LA already. I didn't get the chance to ask her why, because she had already stopped working at the store with us. Now at the store, it was just me and Adrian together with a new girl that I can't remember her name. What I know is that she has been flirting with Adrian ever since and it's getting on my nerves.

"What would you like to get?" A young lady, probably my age or older, asked, standing in front of our table. She doesn't look too excited to be here, but she forces a small smile, trying to appear friendly.

"Cheeseburger and some fries with coke," Adrian orders.

The lady turns to me and I speak, "I'll have the same."

She nods and heads the same way she came. The door opens and Adrian's father walks in. Adrian and his father share almost everything. One look at both of them and you'll know that they have the same blood running through their veins. I didn't notice the similarities when he came to the house.

Aunt Destiny isn't aware of this meeting and I'm sure if she is, she'll lose her shit. She's still around for the rest of the week and most likely till next week.

Adrian's father notices us almost immediately and a small smile is on his face as he walks toward us. Adrian looks up when his father is now standing in front of us.

"Son, I'm so glad you agreed to meet with me." he takes the seat opposite Adrian. "And this must be your friend."

"Yeah. This is Funke, my best friend," Adrian introduces as he motions to me.

"Hi, nice to meet you," I give a small smile with a nod, choosing not to go for the handshake. I freak out a lot when I'm around the opposite gender, especially the older ones.

"Nice to meet you too, I'm George," he stretches out his hand and when I don't shake it, he awkwardly drops it back. "So, son, how have you been?"

"Please call me Adrian, and I've been fine," Adrian answers, his voice not so welcoming.

I'm slightly taken aback by his sudden tone. I thought he was excited to see his father. Why is he suddenly cold towards him?

George is shocked just as I am, but it doesn't change the tone of his voice. "That's great. How's Nigeria?"

The waitress from earlier reappears, but this time with our food on the tray in her hands. She sets the plates in front of us and asks what Adrian's dad would like. I don't hear it though because I'm too focused on figuring out what is going on with Adrian.

When the waitress disappears again Adrian speaks, "Nigeria is okay. How have you been? And your new life without your first family? Is your new wife treating you well?"

George's mouth drops, and I stare at Adrian in shock. What is going on?

"You know I never understood why you left," Adrian puts a fry in his mouth before picking up the burger. "Why don't we start from there before you ask me how I've been? Make me understand and maybe, just maybe, I'll give you a real chance." He takes a large bite from his burger.

I know there is a mean side to Adrian, but this is way more than I ever expected from him. His face holds no emotions as he chews on his food, waiting for his father to speak. I suddenly start feeling bad for the man. This is surely not what he was expecting.

George's drink arrives and when the lady leaves, he stammers, "I-I-I am sorry for–"

Adrian cut him abruptly. "I don't need you to apologize. Just tell me why you left."

241

I keep my mouth sealed as I eat my food uncomfortably. This is super awkward and kind of scary. I've never seen Adrian like this before.

George takes in a deep breath before letting it out, "when your mum was pregnant with you, it was unplanned. I wasn't ready to be a father and neither was she ready to be a mother. Because of her spiritual background, we got married quicker than I had planned and we started a new life together. When you were born, I was overwhelmed. I didn't know what to do and how to be a good father, but I kept trying. When you were five your mum and I hit a very rocky road and I snapped, I couldn't do it anymore so I left, and went looking for greener pastures hoping that someday I could make it enough to take care of you and your mum."

"And how did that turn out for you?" Adrian eats the last of his burger.

"I was able to get back on my feet and I tried reaching out to your mum, but she didn't let me in. I tried so hard to come back into your life, but she wouldn't let me. She rejected all the money I sent and sent back every gift I sent. I tried, son, I did. I know that doesn't justify what I did, but I hope you can give me a chance here and I promise I won't disappoint you."

Adrian says nothing else as he finishes his food and his drink. That was quick. George nervously plays with the straw of his drink as he waits patiently for Adrian to say something to him.

"I stopped hating you a long time ago, just couldn't figure you out. Look, I think I just need some time and space. Don't call me or text me, I will." Adrian looks at me for the first time since he started talking to his dad and I give him an encouraging smile.

"Alright, take all the time you need. I'll always be here." He stands up and reaches into his pocket, then drops some money on the table. "Take care son and it was great meeting you, Funke," he gives a swift nod before walking out.

"I wasn't expecting what just happened," I tell Adrian when his father is now out of sight. I'm done with my food, just sipping my coke.

"I'm sorry about that," he apologizes, taking my hand in his.

"It's fine Adrian. I understand," I tell him truthfully.

"Thank you for being here with me." I'm glad to have the Adrian I love back.

"Anytime."

We talk for a little while about things not concerning our parents until we decide it is time to leave. I also have to see my therapist today. I'm not too excited about it, but I have to deal with it.

Lagos

Chapter Thirty

I walked side by side with my mother. I was clueless about what she wanted to speak to me about, but I was willing to listen to her.

Our flight to Chicago was in a few days and we were all busy getting ready for the trip. I wasn't so excited about changing locations and environments, but the doctors and every other person said it was the best thing for me. I agreed that a change of environment would be good for my mental health, but a total move out of the country for a year scared me a little. It was out of my comfort zone. My mother thought it was because this was my first time traveling out of the country and I feared making new friends and meeting new people, but it wasn't entirely true.

I simply hated change that was so drastic and could change the course of your life, to change your personality.

Mum halted and so did I. "How are you?" She asked.

Her random question confused me. It was strange that she asked me to take a walk with her, so asking how I am made my confusion worse. "I'm fine," I paused. "What is going on?"

She sighed and continued walking, and I had no other choice but to follow her. We walked in silence for another two minutes before she walked into a restaurant on the other side of the street and I followed her.

The restaurant wasn't crowded, so we found a booth by the French windows. She ordered chicken for both of us and a can of malt for herself while I ordered a bottle of coke.

"Mummy, what is going on?" Her silence was making me uneasy.

"Nothing dear, I just wanted to spend some quality time with you." She smiled.

"Mum, this is more than just spending some quality time with me. What is going on?" She had this sad look on her face, like the dam in her eyes was going to give way soon. She opened her mouth to speak, but the waitress brought our chicken and drinks over. I waited till the waitress had gone before probing mum for answers.

"Did anything happen?" Her sad face was slowly rubbing off on me and I felt like crying too.

"No," she opened her can of malt and dropped the straw into it. She took a sip. "I just wanted to apologize for everything. None of this would have happened if I wasn't negligent of you or if I had just believed you and paid more attention."

I sighed in relief. This wasn't the first time she was apologizing, but this time around, there was something different about it.

"I want to change Funke, I do." She stretched her hand forward on the table, and without waiting for her to ask, I placed my hand in hers. "Please give me a chance to do better." The tears didn't fall, but I could see them gathering in her eyes.

"I don't have a choice anyway," I said, hoping she would laugh, and she did. I laughed with her. "You will away have a chance to do better."

Her smile widened now, but the tears rolled from her eyes. I reached into my purse and took out my handkerchief to give to her. She took it and wiped her eyes.

I waited till she had stopped crying before asking a question I had always needed an answer to. "Why did you marry Seyi?"

I remembered that shortly after she married him, I had asked her that question, but the answer she gave me was, "I love him and he loves me." As a child, I had no other option but to suck it up. Deep down, I always knew there was something more to it.

"Funke, he was the sweetest man I had ever met." She said with a small smile before a frown took over.

"Sweeter than Uncle Jaxon?" I cut in.

"The reasons I and Jaxon's relationship didn't work out is something I don't have the liberty to tell you." She took another sip of her malt.

My coke was getting warm, but I didn't care because I was so interested in hearing everything that my mother had to tell me and I didn't want any distractions.

"Why?"

SAVING HER

She just smiled before speaking again. "I met Seyi at a conference in Abuja and we hit it off pretty fast. He was kind, caring, told the best jokes, and was a total gentleman to me. Unlike other men, he didn't care that I had an eight-year-old daughter." She laughed lightly before continuing to speak. "When he asked me to marry him, I didn't think too much about it because I had been single for so long already and I was ready to be a wife. That was why when you had told me how you felt about him, I flagged you down because he had shown me a side of him that made me believe he was a saint and couldn't hurt a fly." She started crying again, and I didn't move or do anything, just waited for her to get herself together. I knew she had so much more to say, and I was patient and ready to listen.

"When he first hit you, I noticed the faint bruise on your neck. I asked him what happened to you and he told me he did not know. I had my guesses but naïve me still believed that he couldn't hurt a fly. As the years rolled by, I noticed how your demeanor had changed. You weren't as happy as you were before I got married, but I thought it was all a teenage phase and that you'd grow, but I was wrong." She paused. "I should have paid more attention. I should have asked questioned you when I felt something was off, I should have…"

I reached for her hand and squeezed it lightly. "Mum, there's no need to wallow in the past. Now you know better, do better."

She nodded. "You're right, I'll do better. I love you don't forget that."

"I love you too, mum."

Chicago

Chapter Thirty One

"Adrian," I shake him to get his attention. He has been looking back and forth ever since we stepped into the airport.

We are heading back to Nigeria now, for good.

We are starting college in two weeks and my visa is to expire next week, so we might as well leave now. We have to get ourselves ready for college.

It's been a year in Chicago, and I feel a lot better about myself. At least my therapist says I'm good to go. I stopped seeing her two months ago, but she still calls to check up on me once in a while. Talking to strangers for the first time is still difficult for me, older males especially.

Makes me wonder how I intend to cope on campus, but I guess it is one step at a time.

Adrian raises his hand and waves at someone in the distance. I look in that direction and I notice Adrian's father running toward us. I've gotten accustomed to seeing him around. His company isn't that bad.

Adrian's mum didn't take his coming back into their lives lightly. She threw a fit when she learned that Adrian and I had lunch with him after she clearly stated that she didn't want him around. It took a lot of convincing not only from me and Adrian but from my mum too.

Speaking of my mum, I tolerate her better now. It's not the best relationship, but it's the best I can give her now. Adrian isn't too comfortable with its current state, but he understands completely.

"Sorry I'm late son, the workload in the office was so much," Adrian's dad says as he stands in front of us, panting.

"It's fine, you're here now," Adrian beams, happy to see his father.

His dad grins, "Funke, how are you?"

"I'm fine," I smile. "I'll leave you too to talk," I step away from them.

George had to make time to see his son off at the airport. We won't be seeing him for a while. I don't mind, at least someone is seeing us off. They announce our flight through the speakers and I look back at Adrian and his dad. They hug each other and I can see the emotions in Adrian's eyes. I hardly see him get emotional like this.

They finally pull away, and I walked toward them. "That's our flight," I nod to the line that is gradually getting longer.

"I hope to see more of you, Funke," George says, stretching out his hand, which I take, unlike the first time we met.

"Of course," I tighten my bag over my shoulder and Adrian links our hands.

"See ya," he waves before turning around and leading us to the line.

He keeps looking over his shoulder till we can't see him again. When we finally get on the plane Adrian still looks uneasy, so I take his hand.

"You can always get off the plane." I nod to the exit.

He shakes his head. "No, I'll be fine."

I look out the window. I love the window seat. The seatbelt sign comes on and an air hostess comes around, telling us to buckle up and all that. I buckle up and feel Adrian hold my hand. He doesn't like it when we take off. I don't like it either, but I can bear it better compared to him.

Not until we are in the air and free to take off our seatbelts does Adrian let go of my hand. I take out the magazine and start flipping through the pages. This is going to be a long flight.

Lagos

Chapter Thirty Two

When I take the first step down the jet stairs, the fresh air hits my face and I smile. We just landed in Nigeria and let me tell you, I am exhausted.

Someone bumps into me, causing the bag I'm holding to drop. I look up at the person. It's the lady from the cinema months ago. She doesn't look too different and her boyfriend is with her.

"Sorry about that," I apologize and bend down to pick up our bags. She picks mine while I pick hers and we exchange them.

"Wait, I know you," she says, giving me a calculating look.

I shrug. I didn't know what to say.

"You're the lady I met at the cinema some months ago. I commented on your hair," she remembers and grins.

"That is correct," I nod.

"Wow, I'm Victoria. You can call me Riya, nice to meet you," she stretches out her free hand, which I shake. I knew her name would be Victoria.

"Funke, nice to meet you too." I'm surprised that she doesn't introduce her boyfriend.

"Is he your boyfriend?" she leans closer so Adrian doesn't hear what she says.

I look at Adrian and he looks impatient, his foot tapping on the floor like he normally does when he gets impatient.

I shake my head, "no. Is he yours?" I point to the guy behind her.

"No," she shudders.

"Okay, that is not the expression I was expecting," I chuckle.

"Well, it's complicated. But the time we met at the cinema, we were dating." At that, the guy turns to look at me.

"Andrew, this is Funke, Funke, this is Andrew," she introduces us.

"Hi," I wave at him. "And this is Adrian," I introduce Adrian, and he sends her a small wave.

We continue our walk into the airport. Now only a handful of passengers are still around.

"So are you Nigerian?" Riya asks. Her voice still holds that same confidence and smoothness from months ago and her accent `is just the icing on the cake.

"Yeah, you?" They should award me for having a conversation with a stranger for this long without making a fool of myself.

"Mixed, my dad is American." She says.

"So, what are you doing here?"

"My family is moving here and they want me to go to college here so," she shrugs.

"What college?" I am curious about her. She seems interesting and I think we can be good friends.

"UI, University of Ibadan," she rolls her eyes, "What about you? Are you in college?"

My mouth drops. "UI. well, I guess fate brought us together. I'm starting UI this next semester." I guess I've made a new friend.

"Oh my God," she squeals. "You hear that Andrew? I've got a new friend so you can disappear from my life."

Andrew rolls his eyes and I laugh. "I like you already," I nudge her.

She laughs, "What's your course?"

"European studies, you?"

"English Studies."

I guess I'm starting college on a fresh page.

Adrian

Even the strong have demons

Chicago

The Death Of Me

Change seems to love to mock me. I've watched my entire life and that of my best friend, Funke, change faster than I could blink in a year. The pain I feel is a constant reminder that I can't change everything and that sometimes I just have to let life happen. I had to watch her go through everything she went through, and all I could do was sit back and watch. I felt useless. She tells me my presence and constant encouragement is enough for her, but it doesn't feel like it. I wish I can do more than just be a shoulder to cry on. She deserves happiness in her life and now I can't even make her as happy as she should be.

I'm stupidly and madly in love with her and it hurts that I can't be with her in how we want because I don't want to hurt her and now I'm pushed to the friend zone because some bastard couldn't keep his urges to himself. I want to kill that man with my bare hands and then set him on fire. He deserves to rot in jail for the rest of his life, and he certainly doesn't deserve a place with the rest of the world.

I look down at her sleeping figure on my chest and I reach out to tuck a loose strand of her curly hair behind her ears. She stirs in her sleep and lifts her leg higher, now closer to my waist, her left knee resting on my crotch.

This girl is going to be the death of me.

I pull her closer to me and slowly lift her leg so it is now resting on my thighs instead. She unconsciously leans into me, her arms wrapping tighter around my waist and her head now laying on my chest instead of my arm.

"I promise to make you happy Funke, always just please don't leave me," I place a lingering kiss on her forehead. "Please."

I feel my phone vibrating on the bed beside me so I quickly pick it up, stopping the vibrations first so it doesn't wake Funke up before looking at the caller ID.

My father.

I swipe my right thumb across the screen and press the phone to my ear. "Hey, dad."

"Son? Are you alright?" He sounds worried.

"Yeah I am, I just don't want to wake Funke up," I tilt my head to the side.

"Oh, your girlfriend. How is she?"

I look down at Funke. "She's not my girlfriend."

"Come on, it's obvious."

"Nothing's obvious, dad. Just stop talking about it," I roll my eyes. "Why did you call?"

He goes silent and when I think the call has disconnected, he speaks again. "It's William's birthday tomorrow and he'll be hosting a little party or something. It'll be–"

"No," I don't want him to finish his sentence because I already know where he is headed.

"But son–"

"Stop, I don't want to hear it." I grit my teeth.

"Why? He's your brother," from the tone of his voice, it's obvious he doesn't like where this conversation is going. I don't like it too.

"Half," I correct. "Half-brother. Besides, they don't want me there, you don't want me there. I'm pretty sure you're just doing this to look like you care. You can't fool me, dad," I scoff.

"Son, you're gravely mistaken. I want you there, they want you there and we all want you there."

"Save it. I'm not coming." Funke stirs again. "I have to go," I hang up without waiting for a reply.

"You do know that man truly loves you," Funke's groggy voice makes me freeze.

She moves her head so her chin is resting on my chest, her brown and grey eyes are staring at me, judging me.

"Yeah, whatever," I roll my eyes. "Did you hear everything?"

Her head bobs up and down and I groan. "You weren't supposed to."

She sits up abruptly, taking her warmth with her, "but I did."

"Don't start." I sit up too, my back resting on the headboard of the bed.

"Don't start what?" She scoffs, "I'm just worried about you, Adrian. It'll be great if you go for whatever it is he's inviting you over for. I'll go with you if you want."

"It's William's birthday party," I tell her.

"Great a party," her eyes light up. "Come on, don't be a buzz kill. We don't have to spend so much time there, just pop in and out."

"Fine, but only because you asked nicely." I finally give in and she squeals. The effect this woman has on me is wild.

"Trust me Adrian, you won't regret this." She touches my arm before standing up and walking out of the room.

I run my hand through my hair and face. This is difficult, having my dad around and even hanging out with him. Mum doesn't approve, but right now, what she thinks is the least of my worries. We've had lunch a few times and most of the time it's because Funke pushed me to. It's not a bad thing, but when he brings his new family into the equation, it irks me.

When my dad left me and my mother, he met a lady and he got her pregnant. They didn't marry immediately, but he stuck around with her, something he never did with mum and me and he fell in love with her. After she gave birth to Williams, they got married and now they have two more kids. The second is a girl, Tiffany and she's twelve and the last, Benjamin is seven. Dad tells me a lot about them and how much he loves them. This isn't the first time he's invited me over. He keeps telling me that even his new wife and his other kids want me over too, but I keep rejecting his offer. I'm not ready to face them.

Being with them is going to be a reminder of how I can never get what they have because my father is a coward who couldn't face his responsibilities. I can never get a happy family, one where my dad loves my mum, I can't hear him tell her how much he loves her every morning and how beautiful she looks when she dresses up or how proud he is of her when she gets back from work, I can never get that again and he expects me to come over and watch him with his new family, loving them like I want him to love me and be happy and smiling with them? He's kidding.

But since Funke offered to go with me, then that's fine. I'll try not to mess things up and go. It may not be as bad as I think.

SAVING HER

Chicago

Bad Dinners & Awkward Moments

It is bad.

The air in the room is stiff and I can see everyone trying not to make things awkward. The only time Funke's hand had left mine was when we had to use both hands to eat. I'm holding onto her like she is my life support. She is carrying a majority of the conversations despite her bad social skills and I can't be more grateful and also proud of her for growing so much.

Dad had asked if I could come earlier to have dinner with them before the party, so we were currently at the dining table. The food is great actually; I think that is one thing keeping me sane at the moment.

"So Adrian, your dad tells me you play basketball," Brittany, dad's new wife, says.

I take a sip of my water before speaking, "yeah."

"That's great. Liam loves playing basketball, too. Maybe you guys can get to play together sometime."

I set my gaze on Williams and he has a tight smile on his face as he stares back at me. He is eighteen, two years younger than me, but because of everything that has happened, we're starting college at the same time. Sadly, he looks so much like my dad and since I look like my dad; we look alike. The same brown hair and brown eyes, the only difference is, he's shorter than I am and he has freckles he got from his mum scattered over his nose and cheeks, giving him this cute look.

I nod, "sure only if Williams is up for it." I shrug casually, still maintaining eye contact with Williams.

Everyone at the table joins me to look at the birthday boy, waiting for his reply.

"No problem," he finally answers and breaks eye contact, so I look away.

Funke squeezes my hand tighter under the table and I look at her with a smile to tell her I'm fine. She smiles back softly and goes back to her food.

"Son, how's your college application coming? Any news?" Dad asks. He has been quiet for most of the night.

"Yes, we got in. In less than a month, we should be leaving." I answer before filling my mouth with food.

"I'm so proud of you, son. It's that school, UI right?"

I nod, not being able to talk with food in my mouth.

"What are you studying?" Tiffany speaks for the first time since we've sat at the table.

"Theatre Arts," I answer, looking at her.

She was the carbon copy of her mother, with red hair, shiny blue eyes, and freckles. She seems to be the shy one in the family.

"What about your girlfriend?" She asks.

"European studies," Funke speaks at the same time. I say, "she's not my girlfriend."

Everyone in the room looks between both of us, taking in the information we both dumped on them.

"So she's single," Williams says with a smirk. I know that smirk. He's going to take a shot at hitting on Funke.

"Try shit and you'll regret it," I glower at him.

He gulps and sinks into his seat. "I was joking, bro."

"Better be." I look back at Funke, who looks like she is going to burst with embarrassment.

Shit, I fucked up. But I can't sit there and watch him try anything stupid.

I lean towards Funke and whisper in her ear, "I'm sorry."

She shivers slightly and nods, "it's fine."

"Son, you might want to tone it down on the language next time. There are kids on the table," Dad cautions.

"I'm sorry," I apologize.

"If there will be a next time," Funke mumbles under her breath, and I wouldn't have heard her if I wasn't still leaning into her.

I smirk and sit back. We finish our meal in silence and Funke and Brittany go into the kitchen to get dessert. A minute after, the pair walk back in with pies in their hands.

When I have a better look and the aroma of the pie hits my nose, I shudder.

"I'm sorry, is this strawberry pie?" I direct my question to Brittany.

"Yea," she nods.

Funke and I share a look. "I'm allergic to strawberries," I look at my dad. "He didn't tell you?"

"Oh God," he face palms himself. "I'm sorry son, I didn't even know that's what she had prepared." He gives me an apologetic look.

"But I asked you if he had any allergies I should know about." Brittany sounds pissed. I would be pissed if I were her.

"I guess it slipped my mind. I'm sorry." Dad gives her the same apologetic look.

"Don't worry, mum, we'll both sit this one out," Williams sets the napkin that was once on his lap on the table. "I wanted to show him the basketball court anyway," he stands up and beckons for me to follow him.

I look at Funke to see if she is okay with me leaving her there, and she nods. I shrug, "alright."

SAVING HER

I follow Williams to the basketball court at the back of the house. He stops walking when we are a little distant from the house. He picks a ball that was lying on the floor. "You hate me, don't you?"

His boldness takes me by surprise. "No, I don't." I catch the ball as he throws it to me.

"Are you sure?" His accent is stronger than mine since he's lived in Chicago all his life.

"If I hate you, I wouldn't be here right now." I throw the ball back at him and he catches it with ease.

He smirks. "fair enough." He bounces the ball twice. "I'm sorry about dad."

"Don't apologize for his flaws. It's not your fault."

"It kind of is," he passes the ball. "If my mum wasn't pregnant with me, he probably wouldn't have married her."

"You weren't the one who told him to stick his dick in your mum and forget to be careful." I bounce the ball before making an aim for the basket. It rolls around the rim a little before falling right through the net.

He chuckles before clearing his throat, "if you put it that way. I'm also sorry for what I said about Funke. That was stupid of me."

"That also is fine, but take my threat seriously, though."

He laughs, throwing his head back, "oh I will. But in all honesty, are you sure you guys aren't dating?"

I suck in a breath while rolling the basketball between my hands. "It's complicated."

"Better un-complicate it because it'll be difficult to convince people that you guys aren't dating, especially when you guys give each other lovey-dovey eyes."

"Jesus," I gasp and pass the ball to him.

"You like her, don't you?" He aims for the net and I watch the ball fly in.

"Yeah," I nod.

"Then tell her already," he passes the ball to me again.

"She knows. Like I said, it's complicated."

"Alright. My friends are coming over next tomorrow, we usually play basketball together. You want to come over, meet them?"

I shrug, "maybe."

"I'll text you when," he smirks and makes an aim for the ball in my hand.

We play together, dribbling and scoring against each other. I give him credit, though. He's good, maybe as good as me.

"Boys!" I hear dad call us in. Williams drops the ball and we walk back into the house together.

"Please tell me you guys are staying for the party," Brittany says as we join them in the living room.

I look at Funke. If she wants to stay, then that's fine by me. Talking with Williams has somehow made me relax a little.

"We'll stay for a little while," Funke smiles.

"Uh Williams," I call his attention while handing him the Starbucks gift cards I got him as a gift. "I hope you like coffee."

Since it was last minute, that was the only thing I had in mind to get. I just hope he likes it.

"Like? I love it!" He examines the cards and a grin slowly breaks out on his face. "Man, this is amazing, thank you. How did you know?"

"Honestly, I just hoped you'd be a coffee drinker," I shrug.

"I appreciate man and thanks for coming," he turns to Funke. "Thank you, too."

"Anytime," she smiles at him.

Guests start flooding the house and an hour after Funke and I decide we have to leave, so we say our goodbyes and I drive us home.

Chicago Cold Showers

"I'm proud of you Adrian," Funke says from beside me on the couch. We are currently watching a movie that I didn't bother myself to know the name but the plot so far is interesting.

"You sound like my mum." I look up from my phone to look at her. This is one of those moments that I unapologetically appreciate her beauty: her heterochromia, her curly hair which she usually has in a bun, her body, and her soul; she's beautiful.

She chuckles, "alright but I'm proud of you."

"What suddenly makes you say that?" I lock my phone screen, now giving her my full attention and myself a better chance to soak in the beauty before me. I love the way her mouth moves when she speaks or how you can see the seriousness in her eyes when she enters her 'no jokes' mode. "You didn't fuck up so much last night." She gives me one of her signature smiles and I feel my heart beating faster than normal.

"So I fucked up?"

"A little, but it's fine since I expected it." She shrugs.

"So don't you think I deserve a reward for not fucking up badly?" I smirk and lean closer to her. I know we both agreed to wait, but God, it's so hard to resist her. Her very existence calls to my soul.

She avoids looking at me, now fixing her gaze on the TV. She is biting her smile.

"Come on, give me some sugar." I hold her by her waist and pull her to me. I just need a taste of her lips one more time.

She giggles and tries to push me off with her hand on my chest. I lean in and capture her lips with mine. She kisses me back instantly, wrapping her hands around my neck and pulling me to her.

You shouldn't be doing this.

I push the nagging voice to the back of my head. I don't need negativity right now. All I need is Funke, so I focus on her lips on mine, her hands all over my chest, hair, and shoulders.

She pulls me down as she rests her back on the couch. I follow her lead, never for once breaking the kiss.

"I want you, Adrian," she says in a low voice as she nibbles on my bottom lip.

I pull back and stare at her eyes. Her grey eye looks darker than usual. She doesn't know what she's saying. Lust clouds through her mind. I know my actions right now had led her on, but I didn't want to have all of her right now. We still have the time for that and when that time comes, I won't hold myself back.

"No, you don't." I shake my head and pull away from her, the sensible part of me finally waking up.

She holds me back down. "I know what I'm saying." Her hand trails down to my waist and I hold her hand to stop her. Hurt flashes in her eyes and a scowl takes over her face.

"You're just blinded by lust, Funke," I pull from her grip but still hold her hand. "I'll hurt you and you know that."

She rolls her eyes, "enough with that, you won't hurt me. I want you Adrian, and that's all that matters." She trails her hand over my arm, but pauses. "Unless you don't want me."

I don't speak because I know how this is going to end. I'll say I want her and she'll tell me to prove it. She will probably try to kill herself again when I disagree.

I close my eyes instead and take in deep breaths.

"You don't want me," she lets go of my hand and I hear her stand up from the couch. Seconds after,I hear her heavy footsteps retreating up the stairs.

I stand up and follow her, my long strides easily catching up with her. I stop her room door from slamming in my face, pushing the door open. In two long strides, I'm mere inches from her, so I pull her to me with her back pressed against my chest. "I want you, Funke," I whisper in her ear and I hear her suck in a breath.

"Prove it," she turns around to face me.

I shake my head, "Funke, please stop. Don't make me do this."

"Prove it, Adrian, prove that you want me," she trails her hand up and down my arm.

"I don't need to prove a fucking thing. I want you and you know it, it's ju–"

She presses a finger to my lips, "that's exactly what I want you to do, fuck me."

Where the heck is the shy and sensible Funke when I need her?

"I will not fuck you, Funke, not yet." I pull her closer to me, expelling any gap that was between us. "Do you understand?"

"Fine," she pushes me and walks to her bathroom. "Maybe I'll just fuck myself then, and I'll have fun without you." She slams the bathroom door behind her.

It takes two seconds for the meaning of what she said to sink in. My eyes widen and I struggle with the door, but she has already locked it. "Funke! Open this door now!" I pound my fist on the door.

I hear her moan loudly and my jaw drops. I am relieved that she isn't trying to physically harm herself, but still furious that she is going to pleasure herself. The mere thought of that is driving me crazy. If she wants to do that, I should watch her.

Her moans get louder and I tire of pounding my fist on the door. I turn around and rest the back of my head on the door. I'll be here if she does something *more* to herself.

For two agonizing minutes, I hear her pleasure herself and suddenly silence ensues. My heartbeat spikes up, beating ten times faster than normal.

"Funke!" I yell once again.

Silence.

"Funke, if you're okay, please say something, do something, please!"

Silence.

Fuck this.

I push my foot on the door and the second time contact it; it falls with a loud bang on the floor.

Anger and relief flood through me when I see Funke resting on the shower wall with a smirk on her face and her hand in between her legs. She's alright, and naked and damn me, but her body is irresistible.

SAVING HER

"Why?" I'm breathing heavily, trying to calm down and also stopping myself from going over to her and claiming her.

"I knew that would get your attention." Her smirk deepens, and she kneads her breast with her other hand.

"Funke stop." My eyes widen. "You know what? I'm out of here." I turn around and walk away.

"You'll miss out on the fun, baby!" She yells after me and I fight the urge to turn back around and take her right there in the bathroom. I shake my head, hoping my sinful thoughts would go away. I shut the room door behind me and rest my back on it before sliding down to the floor.

I sit there till I hear her turn off the shower, walk into her closet to change, then throw herself on her bed before I walk to my room. The bulge in my pants means one thing: I need a cold shower.

Chicago

Bad Friends & Irreversible Mistakes

I watch Funke get down from the car, walk to Lucy's front door and press the doorbell. I once again admire what she's wearing: a yellow dress that has a thin strap and flows to her knees. It doesn't hug her body, but it highlights her curves. She's wearing white sneakers with it.

Lucy finally opens the door and drags Funke inside. I change the gear and drive off. When I get to dad's house, I press the doorbell and wait. Seconds after, a sweaty Williams opens the door. He is wearing basketball shorts and his chest is bare and sweaty. I see they've already started playing.

SAVING HER

"Hey bro, you made it!" He opens the door wider, ushering me in. He's panting as if he had just run a marathon.

"Yeah," I shrug. "I see you guys have started without me."

He walks towards the basketball court at the back of the house, and I follow him. We go through the kitchen today, unlike the other night when we went through the hallway close to the kitchen.

"My guys are just impatient," he chuckles and quickly opens the fridge, takes out two bottles of water, and tosses one to me, which I catch. "You know next time you don't have to use the doorbell, just walk in. It's your house too, you know."

"I don't know about that." I close the door behind me. Before seeing them, I hear them; guys playing basketball, I've missed it. I used to play basketball with my friends back in secondary school.

"Hey, guys, look who's here!" Williams gets everyone's attention and all heads snap towards us.

"This is my half-brother, Adrian. Adrian, this is Henry." He points to a slim, blonde guy. His height is intimidating. "Tim," A guy with black hair, he is probably around my height or slightly taller. "Dakota," I smile at that. Dakota is my childhood friend.

"Hey man, I didn't know it was you this idiot was talking about!" Dakota makes his way over to me and we shake hands before side hugging each other.

Williams pushes Dakota, and Dakota pushes him back before running away from him. "Atty, short for Atticus," Williams continues with the introductions, now pointing to a dark-skinned guy whose hair is curly with a gold tip. "And finally Andrew," the last guy looks familiar. His dreadlocks fall over his face and he looks more muscular than everyone here. His sharp grey eyes quickly give him away. He's the guy Funke, and I saw at the cinema the other night. He was with his girlfriend that night. Now he doesn't seem to recognize me. His mini salute with two fingers proves it. I let it slide and act like I don't know him. I greet the other guys and the game of basketball continues.

When we are all tired and drenched in sweat, some of us sit on the concrete floor while some, like me, sit on the bench outside, gulping down water and wiping our sweats.

"Damn Adrian, you're good. Where did you learn to play like that?" Atty comments, finishing his bottle of water.

"High school, my friends and I used to mess around," I answer.

"You weren't on the team?" Henry asks.

"My friends and I got kicked out of the team," I chuckle at the memory. "Joined the tracks instead, but still fooled around once in a while."

"Ah, I see, little troublemaker," Atty says and everyone cracks up in laughter.

Andrew finally walks back to us. He excused himself to answer a phone call after we finished the game. He sits on the floor beside Atty and gulps down his bottle of water.

"Victoria again?" Henry asks with a barely noticeable frown on his face.

"Yeah, apparently my mum is looking for me." Andrew takes in a breath and slowly exhales.

"I'm jealous of you guys, man," Atty pushes Andrew's shoulders.

"Please, what should you be jealous of? A relationship without sex is useless," Henry says with a scoff.

"You think. A relationship is not all about sex, bro," William pipes in.

I wanted to say those exact words.

"Just because Victoria and I don't have sex doesn't mean it's useless," Andrew now has a scowl on his face.

"Or she's just being mother Theresa and waiting till marriage," Henry says with a mocking laugh. He's the only one who finds this amusing.

"Yeah, and what's wrong with that?" Andrew quirks a brow at him.

"Nothing." Henry raises his hand in mock surrender. "Just saying, at this rate, your balls are probably going to die before you get to fuck her, or maybe I'll just sweep in and show you how it's done."

My eyes widen. I don't think I like Henry. He seems to be the wildest card amongst this group of friends.

"That won't happen," Andrew finally says after a few seconds of silence, his voice filled with distaste and anger.

"Oh really, then prove it bro, fuck her and prove that you're man enough to keep your lady, if you don't I'll have to jump in." Henry has this crazy smirk on his face that irks me.

I look at Williams and whisper, "Is this how he is?"

290

"Yeah, that's Henry for you," he nods, whispering back.

"If Andrew agrees to this, he's an even bigger fool," I look at the said Andrew and it looks like he is going to explode with anger.

"Let's see," William shrugs.

"I don't have to prove anything to you." Andrew scoffs and stands up, dusting his basketball shorts.

"Stop being a pussy man, just admit it, you can't get your girlfriend to fuck you," Henry continues, even though Andrew is ready to drop the topic.

A smirk slowly makes its way to Andrew's face, "and if I do just that, what's going to happen?"

"You get to use my car till you leave for Nigeria," Henry is quick to say.

Henry's car must be cool because Andrew's smirk deepens.

"And if you don't by a week before you leave for Nigeria, I get to take her on a date and if I get a taste of that pussy, you don't fight it," Henry adds.

"That will not happen. Get ready to use Uber more often," Andrew chuckles and tosses the basketball on the floor at Henry.

He catches the ball. "We'll see."

This will not end well for Andrew. Either he loses the bet or Victoria finds out about this and dumps his ass. I can just feel it.

I turn to Williams as the others stand up to start a game. "Andrew lives in Nigeria or what?" I choose not to ignore the comment Henry made about Nigeria.

"No, but he's moving there for college, him and his girlfriend, Victoria," he tells me.

"Oh, they're Nigerians?" We walk toward the others.

"Mixed," he catches the ball that is thrown at him and that is the end of the conversation.

The couple must love each other so much to decide to study in Nigeria and go together. I hope he isn't studying at UI because I can't imagine the idea of studying in the same school as a guy like him. He's an asshole and his girlfriend doesn't deserve him.

"So Williams, your half-brother, huh?" Andrew passes him the ball. "What happened? Your dad forgot where to stick his dick at?"

At that moment, Williams passes me the ball and I freeze after my head processes the words that left his mouth.

SAVING HER

Though his words are true, it is still hurtful and disrespectful to both me and Williams. I had commented in that fashion the other night, but it was a lot more respectful. I respected his mum with the comment and it wasn't offensive to Liam, this was just downright disrespectful. Even if I disrespected my dad with my comment, he's my dad. It's different when it comes from an outsider, especially if they don't know the full story.

The ball leaves my hand, then loud cheering. The opposing team got hold of the ball and scored. That was the least of my worries right now.

Williams is frozen too, and slowly every other person stops moving to look at all three of us. They all heard the comment and any sensible person would have known that Andrew had just crossed a line.

"What did you say?" I make my way over to him.

"Chill man, I was just joking," he chuckles dryly.

"Joking? You call that a joke?" Williams joins me and we both make our way to Andrew.

"Alright man, I'm sorry, I didn't mean it like that," Andrew takes a step back.

I stop walking, deciding I have had enough of William's friends. "I'm out of here," I turn to leave and hear Williams' and Dakota's voices calling me back.

"Bro, wait up!" Williams catches up with me and places his hand on my shoulder automatically, making me stop walking, too.

"Your friends are disgusting," I spit.

He sighs. "With what you saw today, I have to agree with you."

"How do you manage with them?"

"I have no idea." He looks at the door we just walked through. "Don't leave just yet," he pleads.

"I can't handle one more minute with them. I'm sorry, Williams, but I have to go." I shake my head.

He sighs again. "Alright, we'll talk later. I'm sorry about them."

"It's fine." I move but stop to say something. "If you can still stop Andrew with that crazy bet, please do, because I can see it. He's going to lose the bet or Victoria's going to find out and that'll be the end. He's going to lose her forever."

"I know, I'll do what I can." He touches my shoulder. "Say hi to Funke for me."

SAVING HER

"I will." I force a smile before walking out of the house.

Chicago

Dreams & Hopes

"How was your day?" Funke throws herself on my bed, now freshly showered. The scent of her Vanilla scented soap reaches my nose and I nearly melt into a puddle. I just want to hold her close to me and breathe in her scent.

I remember the events of today and decided not to tell her. I should keep it to myself. We'll probably never see those guys again. "Not as good as I expected, but okay," I choose to say, my gaze not leaving my computer. "How was yours?"

"It was fun…" I listen as she goes on and on about what happened while she was at Lucy's house. She was excited and I became grateful for not telling her how my day went. I would have spoilt her mood.

When I had gotten back home, my mind kept on playing all the conversations in my head. I felt like strangling Andrew and Henry, and I had pity on Victoria. I wish there was a way to tell her what was going on. When Funke was ready to come home, I had to drive out again to pick her up.

We had dinner together, and I had gone up for a shower. After that, I picked up my computer and continued writing the script I was writing before. Writing scripts was something I always did, and I loved it. I have three completed. I hope my dreams of being a movie director and scriptwriter can come true.

"Lucy's mum is inviting us for dinner before we go back to Nigeria," Funke tells me.

"Sure, just ask when." I close my computer and set it aside, ready to get some sleep.

"What's bothering you, you've been distant ever since we got back." Funke sits up and crosses her legs under her, now facing me.

"Nothing." I shake my head and cross my arms.

297

"Is it your dad? Did something happen today?" Her eyes hold empathy.

"No," I sigh. "It's just that a lot is going on." I run my hand through my hair and over my face.

"Everything will fall in place," she holds my hand and came to sit beside me. "Everything."

"Thank you for being here." I bring her hand to my lips and kiss the back of her palm.

"Thank you," she says with a smile.

"Have you spoken to your mum?"

"Nah," she shakes her head, and her face changes.

"Why? She's your mum, you know?" I don't want to force anything on her since I can't say much for myself when it comes to my dad.

"How often do you call your dad?" she fires back. I knew she was going to go there.

I keep shut. She has a point, though. A deafening silence slices through the air and I'm the one to break it. "We can do better if we both try."

"I know." She closes her eyes and takes in a deep breath before slowly releasing it.

SAVING HER

"Come here," I pull her in for a hug, and after, she rests her head on my shoulder while I wrap my arms around her body.

Antsy. Anxious. Uncomfortable.

It isn't helping that all I can do is bite my nails as I scan the airport. Funke keeps telling me to relax.

If dad doesn't show up in a minute, we'll have to leave or we'll miss our flight. On the way to the airport, he called to tell me he'll meet me at the airport since he couldn't meet us at home.

After Funke and I made that agreement, I had put the effort into my relationship with my dad and it was going well. We hung out a few times, and he even showed me his office and explained how things work. Funke, Williams,

Benjamin, Tiffany, and I hung out a few times, too. They're all cool with having me around and I'm pleased to know that.

I finally notice a lock of brown hair running over and I wave at him.

"Sorry I'm late son, the workload in the office was so much," he says when he finally stops in front of us.

"It's fine, you're here now," that's all that matters.

Dad grins, "Funke, how are you?"

"I'm fine," she smiles. "I'll leave you two to talk." She keeps a distance between us, giving us privacy.

"I'm going to miss you," dad says. "You can come study here instead, you know. I'll settle both of you," he briefly looks at Funke.

"This is her dream and mine, too." I also steal a glance at her.

Dad smiles, "alright, I'll always be here if you need me. Come back anytime, to visit or otherwise."

"Of course."

"Take care of your mother, and send my greetings to her," he pats my shoulder. They announce our flight and dad quickly hugs me. "I love you. Always know that."

The right response is at the tip of my tongue, but I fear how it is going to make me feel if I say them. I squeeze my eyes shut and say them either way. "I love you too dad," I pat his back when we pull away from the hug.

All I feel is a sort of satisfaction with myself after, which is the total opposite of what I was expecting. I was expecting to feel weird or grossed out.

"That's our flight," Funke appears and nods to the line that has grown longer.

"I hope to see more of you Funke," Dad stretches out his hand for a handshake which Funke takes, which is progress at least.

"Of course." I reach for her hand and intertwine our fingers.

"See ya," I wave and turn around, taking Funke with me. I keep looking over my shoulder until I can no longer see his head again.

When we get on the plane, Funke takes my hand in hers. "You can always get off the plane," she nods towards the exit.

"No, I'll be fine." I don't know why I'm feeling this many emotions, but I'm feeling it and it's killing me. Something must be wrong with me.

Lagos

College Is Going To Be Fun

"Sorry about that," I hear Funke say and she bends down to pick a bag and then exchanges it with the lady in front of her.

The lady looks familiar.

"Wait, I know you," the lady says.

Funke just shrugs casually.

"You're the lady I met at the cinema some months ago. I commented on your hair."

Now it makes sense. If she's the one, then her boyfriend Andrew must be around. I look around for him and see him a few feet behind. Maybe they're not even dating anymore, but if that's the case, then why are they together?

"That is correct," Funke nods.

"Wow, I'm Victoria. You can call me. Riya, nice to meet you," she offers a handshake, which Funke takes.

"Funke, nice to meet you too."

"Is he your boyfriend?" The lady asks, leaning closer to Funke. She probably thinks I can't hear them.

Funke looks my way and I look away, tapping my foot on the ground so she'd think I was getting impatient.

"No. Is he yours?" Funke is talking about Andrew. I was waiting for that.

"No."

I have to stop myself from laughing out loud. I just knew it, Victoria found out.

"Okay, that is not the expression I was expecting," Funke chuckles.

"Well, it's complicated. But the time we saw at the movies we were dating,"

Andrew finally looks our way. He is avoiding eye contact with me.

"Andrew, this is Funke, Funke, this is Andrew," Victoria starts the introductions.

"Hi," Funke waves. "And this is Adrian," she gestures to me and I send them a small wave. Andrew's gaze meets mine and I smirk. He hurriedly looks away.

"So are you Nigerian?" Victoria asks as we make our way into the airport.

"Yeah, you?"

"Mixed, my dad is American."

"So, what are you doing here?"

Right question Funke.

"My family is moving here and they want me to go to college here."

"What college?" I'll give you a medal for this Funke.

"UI, University of Ibadan. What about you? Are you in college?"

I am shocked. That means Andrew is going to be at the school too. Fuck my life.

Funke looks just as shocked as me. "UI. Well, I guess fate brought us together. I'm starting UI this next semester."

"Oh my God," Victoria squeals. "You hear that Andrew? I've got a new friend so you can disappear from my life."

Ouch. That confirms it.

Andrew rolls his eyes and Funke laughs. "I like you already,"

I fight my laugh.

Victoria laughed. "What's your course?"

"European studies, you?"

"English."

Nice. I just hope Mr. Asshole here will not be in the art faculty too.

Five minutes after, I find out that I can jinx things because Andrew turns out to be in the art faculty too.

With Funke and Victoria becoming friends, I guess I'll have to see Andrew more often. There's nothing I can do but sit and watch.

College is going to be fun.

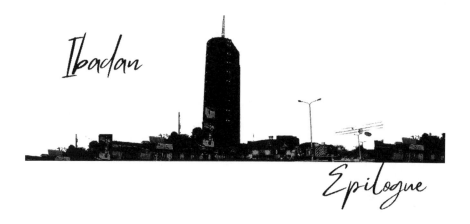

Ibadan

Epilogue

"It's open," I call to whoever is at the door, still focused on using the eyeliner perfectly well.

I hear the door creak open and then shut close. "Are you ready? Victoria's here."

"Almost," I answer, careful not to mess up what I'm doing.

"Be fast," From the corner of my eyes I see him sit on the bed and take up the novel that was lying on the bed. He looks dashingly handsome, as always, in plain blue suit pants and a well-ironed plain black dress shirt. It is matriculation day, meaning the semester is almost over.

First, I'd like to applaud myself for surviving the past three months without a panic attack and without trying to kill myself. I've come close to suicide a lot of times and I've pulled out of it by myself and without Adrian's knowledge.

He never hides the constant fear and worries he feels. Left for him, we would live in the same house, if not that the two-bedroom apartments we could find are too far away from campus. But now we both have our apartments in the same apartment block, his room right beside mine.

He has been making sure I take my medications on time and driving me to my therapist appointments even on days when he's about to pass out. I refused to use my car ever since, despite the constant begging from my mum. If I need to drive, I use Adrian's car and it's way more convenient that way. Saves more fuel.

"How do I look?" I step out of the bathroom and do a little pose for Adrian.

He carefully scans me from head to toe, and when his eyes meet mine, he smiles. "Beautiful." He says and stands up. "Shall we?"

"Yes, we shall." I take my purse from the bed and make sure my eyeglass is in its case and sitting on my table before following Adrian out of the room and locking the door.

It turns out that I have a problem with seeing things from a far distance, so I had to get glasses. I can still drive without them, so it's more for when I'm in class or if I want to read for a long period.

"You didn't tell me we were going with Andrew too," I complain as I see Andrew leaning on his white Venza.

When I first met Andrew, I had nothing against him until Victoria told me what he did and that was when the hate for him grew. Adrian also hates him even before Victoria had told us what happened. At first, I thought maybe Adrian had feelings for Victoria and he was angry that Andrew was there, but after much interrogation; I realized that wasn't the case. I don't know whatever it is, but I will find out, soon enough I hope.

Adrian opens the door for me and I get in, surprised to see Victoria sitting in the back seat and not at shotgun.

"Oh My God, you look stunning in that dress." She gushes.

"Are you even looking at yourself?" I admire her overall look.

I'm wearing a blue spaghetti-strapped body con dress. While she's wearing a red jumpsuit. Her makeup is mild but still visible. I love it. She chuckles and nods to the front of the car where Adrian and Andrew are. Andrew is behind the wheels and the tension between them was undeniable, and Victoria and I found amusement in it.

Since the day we met each other at the airport, we've been inseparable. We have classes together and eat together. The only thing that causes a brief gap is that her apartment is a few blocks away from mine. We're similar in almost everything: we wear the same size of shoes and clothes and we're the same height. We're the same person in separate bodies and slightly distinct personalities.

Coming to the university, I realized that I'm an outgoing person but because of my history at home; I kept more to myself. There are things that Victoria can't say or do in public, but for me, I don't give a fuck.

Adjusting to university life wasn't easy at first, especially still having to find my bearings, but with people around me, it was easier. I'm still figuring out a lot of things about myself, but I don't feel alone. I have Adrian and Victoria.

The campus is packed with people, and unlike Victoria and Andrew, who have an eye out for their parents, Adrian and I don't. Adrian's mum is working today and she can't leave. My mum is, as usual, out of the country. She sent me gifts and money, so tonight we are all going out and having fun.

Victoria and Andrew introduce Adrian and me to their parents. They asked about our parents and we told them what we always tell people. *They are caught up in work.'*

I haven't told Victoria about my family history and I don't have plans to soon. It's not because I don't trust her, but more of the fact that it's a hard topic to talk about. I'm trying to avoid having a panic attack. One day I will tell her, but not now.

After all rituals of the day, we are all taking pictures and my phone rings so I have to excuse myself from my friends.

"Hello?" I do not know who is calling me.

"Funke, it's Uncle Jaxon." That voice, I can recognize it anywhere. It has been thirteen years since I heard his voice and since I spoke to him. Since the day that my mother married Seyi, I haven't seen him or spoken to him.

That day he promised me he was coming back but that while waiting for him to come back that I shouldn't call him or find a way to reach him. I cried my eyes out that day as I watched him drive away, but I told myself that a promise was a promise. He said he was going to come back and he will come back, so I held onto his words.

The first few years were tough, but I pulled through and with time I only remembered him once in a blue moon.

I chuckle and feel the tears welling up in my eyes.

"I'm back. Turn around."

I do, and my smile widens when I see him standing a few feet away from me. It feels like I'm eight again as I run towards him and throw myself on him, not giving a flying fuck who is looking at me.

"You came back." I let the tears fall as I hold on to him like he is my life support.

"I told you I will." He says.

Déjà vu is hitting me like a ton of bricks.

"I missed you. It's been so hard without you. My life has been a mess," I cry, and he holds my shoulders. His eyes are teary too as he looks at me. "I know. I'm sorry I didn't come sooner. Your mum wouldn't let me reach you, no matter how hard I tried. But today I got your number from her."

I hug him again and hold him even tighter, not ready to let go of him.

"I'm sorry I couldn't do anything." It doesn't look like he is ready to let me go, either.

"Funke?" Adrian suddenly appears, causing me to pull away from Uncle Jaxon.

"Adrian," I sniffle, and use my handkerchief to dab my tears away. I'm not using waterproof mascara. "This is Uncle Jaxon."

Adrian is confused for a second or two before his eyes widen and he looks at the said man in front of him. He chuckles and looks at me, then nods. "Good afternoon, I'm Adrian," he stretches his hand forward and Uncle Jaxon takes it in a firm handshake.

After the introductions and greetings, Adrian excuses us and tells me to call him whenever I'm done. I had told Adrian about Uncle Jaxon, so he is the only man Adrian can leave me alone with.

"Your boyfriend?" Uncle Jaxon has on a suggestive smirk.

"No," it is the truth.

"But he likes you." he wiggles his brows and I roll my eyes. "And you like him." He adds.

"Well," I trailed off and avoid his eyes.

"Then why aren't you guys dating?" The one question I hate hearing.

I sigh. "Because he's trying to avoid me trying to kill myself again,"

His smile drops. "That's the wise thing to do. I support him."

"You do?" I frown.

"Yes." He nods. "You need time to heal and get over your past. If you guys start dating, you can't deny that you guys may kiss or cuddle and all that and it will make you remember things you shouldn't, so yes, I support him."

SAVING HER

I bite my bottom lip and nod. It feels like the universe is against me and Adrian being together.

"I'm glad you got the courage to talk to him." He chuckles, and I remember. I chuckle too, but say nothing. "Come on, we have a lot of catching up to do." He beckons for me to follow him, and I do.

His car is different this time. This one is a Lexus, fully tinted also may I add.

Like thirteen years ago, he turns on the car and air conditioning as we talk. He asks for my account number and right in front of me sends a hundred thousand Naira to me. We go to an eatery; we eat and I buy food for my friends. He drives me back to my house and we still sit in the car, talking. When I ask him why he always disappears for years, he sighs heavily.

"You know your mum and I dated back in high school," he starts, and I'm in shock. "So you can imagine my surprise to see her again, unmarried and with a child. I wanted to marry her if not for her, but you because I know what it feels like to grow up without a father."

"I proposed to her, and she said yes. Suddenly she called the wedding off and cut me off completely. She gave specific warnings about you: that she never wanted to see me around you. When you called me that day, I knew I needed to come back to see you, and I did."

"Why did you leave again?" He still hasn't answered the question the way I want him to. "Because, despite my mother's warning, you still came to see me when I was eight. So why did you leave me again?"

"I needed to respect your mother's wishes. She didn't want me around you, and I had to respect that." He answers, and I can't detect a lie in his voice.

"Then why are you here? Is it because of what happened?" I can't shake that thought off.

"I'm here because I keep my promises and I promised I'll see you again. Also, you're over eighteen now, though I still respect your mum's wish, you have the right to choose if you want to see me or not. I was going to reach out to you once you turned eighteen but no matter how hard I tried, your mum kept stopping me but she constantly gave me tabs on you and when she told me that today was your matriculation and she couldn't make it, I knew that this was my chance to come to see you." He explains, and my head bops up and down in understanding.

SAVING HER

I notice the silver band on his finger again. "You're married."

"Yeah, with two kids. A girl and a boy, twins." He tells me and I smile.

"I'm so happy for you." I genuinely say, and he smiles back. "So, are you going to leave me again?" I meant it as a joke, but the look on his face says that I should take his answer seriously.

My smile drops, "no."

"I'm sorry, Funke, but I have to."

"No, you don't have to. You have a choice. I'm not saying you should stay here in Nigeria. All I'm saying is that you shouldn't cut off our communication." I plead and he shakes his head.

"Why are you doing this? Please don't cut me off." I feel my eyes sting again and I let the tears fall, not bothering to wipe them off.

"I'm sorry Funke. I will always look out for you, but you won't see me and you won't be able to talk to me again."

I don't know what comes over me, but with anger; I wipe my eyes and pick up the bag he had given me, together with my purse.

"Goodbye," I try to open the door, but it won't budge.

"Funke wait!" He holds my arm. "Don't leave like this."

I shake my head. "You don't understand. I need you."

"For thirteen years you've been without me, you don't need me. All you need is the fact that I'm always watching out for you, that I promise and you know I always keep my promises." He pulls me into a hug and we stay like that for a minute before he plants a kiss on my forehead and lets go of me. Without another word, I smile at him and he returns it before I walk out of his car. I don't turn back even when I hear his car drive off. He always keeps his promises that I'm sure of.

Adrian asks me how I am, and I tell him everything. I thought I was ready for college before, but now I realize I wasn't. But the moment in my room, as I recall the events of the day to Adrian, I know that this is the moment that I am truly ready for college and the rest of my life ahead.

Made in the USA
Columbia, SC
19 October 2022

68949197R00193